SAVAGE

In 1864, Captain Jeff Savage is tasked with taking down Carver's Raiders, a ruthless bunch of killers who have blasted a bloody path through the Shenandoah Valley. The mission is a failure, and Carver escapes with a handful of men. Two years later, he and his gang rob a bank in Summerton, murdering Savage's wife Amy. Several outlaws escape in the aftermath: armed with their names, Savage sets out to track each one down and exact his revenge . . .

JAKE HENRY

SAVAGE

Complete and Unabridged

LINFORD
Leicester

First published in Great Britain in 2016

First Linford Edition
published 2017

A catalogue record for this book is available
from the British Library.

ISBN 978–1–4448–3449–9

Published by
F. A. Thorpe (Publishing)
Anstey, Leicestershire

Set by Words & Graphics Ltd.
Anstey, Leicestershire
Printed and bound in Great Britain by
T. J. International Ltd., Padstow, Cornwall

This book is printed on acid-free paper

This one is for Sam and Jacob

1

Shenandoah Valley, 1864.

'I want your patrol out here, to the east along the foot of The Blue Ridge Mountains. Apparently, we have reports from our left flank that there are raiders about. The General doesn't want them to get behind us and attack our rear elements,' Colonel Augustus Fellows said, stabbing a thick finger at the map of the Shenandoah Valley. The broad, creased sheet was spread out on the scarred top of a wooden table before him.

Fellows was a career officer. A West Point graduate who stood ramrod erect.

Savage leaned forward to get a closer look. The dull orange light cast by the lantern in the Colonel's tent made it fairly difficult to see.

'Any idea who they are, Sir?' Captain Jeff Savage asked his commanding officer.

Savage was thirty-one and now, in 1864, had been fighting against the Confederate States for two years. In that time he'd been in skirmish after skirmish and a few larger battles. The most notable being the clash at Brandy Station in the early stages of the Gettysburg campaign.

His dark brown eyes had seen things that day no man should have to see in a lifetime. His tanned face was a product of long days in the saddle with his Cavalry troop.

'Word is it's Carver,' Fellows said grimly.

Savage straightened up his six-foot-one, solid built frame and ran a hand through his thick black hair.

'That's all we need,' Savage commented.

John Carver was Texas born and a stone cold killer. He and his raiders rode under the Confederate flag, attacked all things Federal and lined his pockets with the proceeds of his forays. He paid no mind to those he killed in order to achieve results.

Although his deeds were committed under the Confederate flag, the Rebel high command had dismissed his unit as bandits and brigands after one of their raids on a small town in Kentucky the previous year had slaughtered many of its citizens.

'From down your way isn't he?' Fellows inquired.

Savage nodded. 'He's from Texas, yes Sir.'

Savage came from the small town of Summerton, in the Texas hill country. He'd worked as a blacksmith and married a most wonderful young lady after a two-year courtship. A week later, he'd ridden out to join the Union in their fight against the Confederacy.

Amy had understood his decision. Many others had not, but he wasn't the first Texan to ride north to fight under the Union flag. He believed that his country should be a united one, not divided for the sake of helping rich men get richer. And after all, wasn't this the land of the free? How could it be claimed to be that when a race of people was enslaved by the will of others?

Savage came back to the present. 'Sorry Sir, what was that?'

'I said take fifty men from your troop and enough rations for a week,' Fellows repeated. 'Cut back from our present position to the north-east and make sure he's not trying to fall in behind us. Once you reach the base of the Blue Ridge Mountains, head south and ride a parallel course to the column.'

'What kind of numbers were reported, Sir?'

'Last reports were around thirty to forty riders,' Fellows answered. 'There may be less, but err on the side of caution and count on more. Pack extra ammunition.'

'And if we find them?'

'Give them what they deserve, Captain,' Fellows hissed in a low voice. 'Kill them all. Let absolutely none escape.'

'Yes, Sir.'

Savage picked up his Hardee hat from a stool in the corner of the tent and placed it firmly on his head.

'I'll leave at first light, Colonel,' he said. 'If you'll excuse me?'

'Watch yourself out there, Jeff,' Fellows cautioned. 'I'd rather you came back to the regiment alive.'

'I'll do what I can, Sir.'

★　★　★

'Sergeant-Major Hayes, are you there?' Savage called from his position outside a discolored canvas tent.

'Yes, Sir,' a gravelly voice called back. 'I'll be right with you.'

The tent flap drew back and Sergeant-Major Ruben Hayes stepped out into the cool evening air.

The man straightened up and stretched his thick-set frame to its full height of six-four. The orange glow of a nearby campfire cast over his features turned his square-jawed face bronze

He was a no-nonsense man who was reliable in any situation, whether in a crisis or just to get something done.

With Savage's current requirements, Hayes was the ideal person for the job.

'Are we movin' out, Sir?' he asked Savage.

'In a fashion, Rube,' he allowed. 'I want fifty men ready to ride at first light. Designate two of them as scouts. I don't want any surprises where we're goin'. Also, extra ammunition for the men and rations for one week.'

'Where is it we're goin', Sir?'

'There's been reports of Carver's raiders over near the Blue Ridge Mountains,' Savage explained. 'We're goin' to see if they're true or not. And if they are, we're under orders to wipe them out. Every last mother's son.'

'I'll see to it, Sir,' Hayes acknowledged.

'One more thing, Rube. Find Lieutenant Forsythe and have him report to me. He'll be in command while we're gone.'

'Right away, Sir.'

Savage watched as his most trusted man disappeared into the night to set about the tasks he'd been given.

* * *

The Union campfires weren't the only ones to cast an orange glow that night. The sky above the tiny hamlet of Bender's Hollow held a similar hue as many of the town's buildings burned.

Loud screams were accompanied by ribald laughter as men forced their unwelcome advances upon the few remaining women still alive in the town.

Major John Carver, self-appointed, stood in the Bender's Hollow main street and watched his men tear the place apart and start to burn it to the ground.

He was a solidly built man of thirty-seven, stood six-three and had blond hair and evil ice-blue eyes. He was square-jawed and wore Confederate issue butternut gray pants, woolen shirt and a Union blue Major's jacket with insignia to match.

Carver caught sight of a small group of men who had a well-dressed citizen in an awkward half carry half drag action as they crossed the street.

'Sergeant Thomas,' he shouted above the din.

One of the men turned and ran towards him. He stopped in front of Carver and saluted. 'Yes, Sir.'

'Just where are you taking that man?' Carver asked. 'And who is he?'

'That be the mayor, Sir.'

'What did you intend to do with him?'

Thomas, who was a slim man with brown hair and eyes, shrugged. 'Not rightly sure at this time, Sir.'

'Well, whatever it is, get it over with quickly and find the damned banker so we can get into his safe,' Carver snapped impatiently.

'Yes, Sir.'

Carver turned his attention to another four men farther along the street who had emerged from a small home. They dragged a woman behind them, who kicked and screamed with fear.

Behind them followed a man who desperately tried to stop them from molesting the woman. One could only assume that she was his wife.

One of the raiders turned away from the struggling woman, lashed out with a fist and caught the man flush on the jaw. He stood still as the man buckled at his feet. He calmly drew his side-arm then shot the unconscious form in the head before he could recover. The gunshot echoed along the street, blending with all the other noises around the town.

The raider turned his back on the corpse and faced the woman. With hands curled into claws, he grasped the top of her dress as she flailed vainly. He gave it a mighty reef and the bodice tore away which exposed her pale flesh to the waist as she tried desperately to regain her modesty.

A man ran out into the street from a burning building. His clothes burned fiercely and his high-pitched screams drowned out those of the woman. Slowly his screams abated and he fell forward on the road. The sickly-sweet smell of burnt flesh permeated the air around his unmoving form.

For the next thirty minutes, the plunder of Bender's Hollow continued unchecked under the watchful eye of Carver. Businesses were looted then burned. The gunsmith shop was emptied followed by the bank safe.

When the raiders, at last, rode out of town, their magician's trick had transformed the once thriving community into a pyre of burnt buildings and death.

★ ★ ★

A mist hung low and covered the Shenandoah Valley the following morning as the column of cavalrymen made ready to leave camp.

Horses stamped and snorted, keen to be moving. The rattle of pots sounded as cooks prepared hot food for the troops as the rest of the army broke camp to continue their march south.

Savage had almost finished a hot,

bitter cup of coffee when his Sergeant-Major approached.

'The men are almost ready, Sir,' he said and glanced wistfully at the coffee mug.

'Grab yourself a cup, Rube,' Savage said, indicating a spare mug by the small campfire.

'Thank you, Sir. Don't mind if I do.'

Savage smiled as he watched Hayes pour himself a cup. His face grew serious. 'When we leave I want the scouts to ride no more than a mile in front of our column. Tell them I want regular reports.'

Hayes blew on his cup before he answered. 'Yes, Sir. I'll see to it.'

'Everyone has extra ammunition and enough rations?'

'Saw to it myself.'

'Did the men get to eat?'

'Yes, Sir.'

Savage looked about the camp one last time then threw the remains of his coffee onto the fire which caused it to spit and hiss.

'Well then, Rube, let's go and see if we can catch this son of a bitch.'

★　★　★

The mist had burned off and was replaced by bright sunshine by mid-morning. The Shenandoah Valley was transformed from a drab gray landscape to a myriad of color.

Oak, hickory, maple, and chestnuts were the prevalent species that grew throughout the valley. The trees lined the narrow roads and provided a haven for the abundance of wildlife that flourished in and amongst them.

Mid-afternoon saw the column of blue-clad riders on a tree-lined lane. They'd reached the farthest point north-east and now had swung in a southerly direction and rode roughly parallel with the Blue Ridge Mountains.

Savage hipped in the saddle and signaled for Hayes to join him at the head of the column. The Sergeant-Major urged his mount forward and fell in beside Savage.

'There's a town about a mile further on,' he told Hayes. 'We'll set up there for the night and move on again at first light. Establish some pickets when we arrive and swap them every couple of hours.'

Savage was about to say more when a flurry of movement came from up ahead. One of the scouts came riding back, a look of concern etched deep in his face. He drew up in front of the two men.

'What is it, Walsh?' Savage asked.

'The town up ahead, Sir,' Walsh gasped out between deep breaths. 'It's called Bender's Hollow.'

'Yes, I know that trooper,' Savage acknowledged. 'What about it?'

'It's bad, Sir,' Walsh said, shaking his head. 'It's . . . '

The cavalryman's voice trailed away.

'What's bad?' Hayes snapped. 'Come on, out with it lad.'

The scout gave Savage a pained expression. 'You'd best see for yourself, Sir.'

Savage nodded. 'Alright trooper, lead the way.'

Before he rode off to follow the scout, Savage turned to Hayes. 'Take over the column, Rube.'

And with that Savage was gone.

★　★　★

A horrid stench greeted Savage when he rode into the ruin that was Bender's Hollow. The smell was a putrid combination of charred wood, smoke, burnt flesh, and death. The bodies of men and women lay in the street. Unfortunately, even the children had not escaped the same grisly fate.

He came across the corpse of a woman, the bodice of her dress had been torn away. The bottom half was hiked up and she had a bullet hole in the side of her head. Nearby, a man had been tied to a wagon wheel and shot to death. Savage could only guess how long it had taken for him to die from the amount of bullet holes in him.

Even a dog hadn't evaded the massacre.

'Who would do this, Sir?' Walsh asked, his face pale. 'What type of human would do this to women and children?'

'The type of men we're after, Walsh.'

There was movement further along the street and Perry, the other scout appeared. With him was a man who they could see as they got closer, had a stunned expression on his face.

They stopped in front of Savage and Walsh.

'I found this here feller hidin' out the back in some trees,' Perry explained. 'I would have missed him except he moved and a branch snapped.'

Savage looked at him carefully then asked, 'What's your name?'

When he didn't answer Perry said, 'I tried talkin' to him, Sir, but he wouldn't say anythin'.'

Savage nodded. 'I'm not surprised. See if you can find anyone else still alive.'

Perry turned and left while Savage climbed down from his saddle and stood in front of the catatonic man. The sound of hooves came from behind him and the man's eyes widened and he stiffened. He looked poised for flight and Savage grabbed his arm gently.

'Easy there,' he soothed. 'They're my men. They won't hurt you.'

Sergeant-Major Hayes halted the column and dismounted. He stood beside Savage and stared around in disbelief.

'I take it that Carver has been here?' he commented.

'I'm not sure, but if I had to guess, I'd say you were right, Rube.'

'I'd like to have that son of a bitch standin' in front of me,' Hayes swore. He then asked, 'Who's our friend?'

'I don't know, he ain't talking.'

'Sir?' Walsh said. 'Sir, look.'

Savage looked at Walsh then followed his gaze. The street was no longer empty. Townsfolk had started to appear from amongst the charred ruins. Many

16

of their faces reflected the expression that the man who stood beside him wore.

'Rube, find someone who's capable of talkin' and tellin' us what the hell happened here. And have the men dismount and help out any way they can.'

'Yes, Sir.'

2

'They came in not long after dark, Captain,' the man explained in a shaky voice.

His eyes grew large as he remembered the bloody rampage that the raiders had effected. Savage noticed his expression.

'Take your time,' he told the traumatized man.

He'd said his name was Oliver. He was a storekeeper who, by the looks of him, had aged prematurely overnight from the horrifying experience he'd witnessed.

'It was terrible,' Oliver moaned. 'The killing. The senseless killing. The screams, I can still hear them.'

'Who was it?' Savage asked, wanting confirmation of his suspicions.

Oliver's face changed to a mask of hatred as he looked into Savage's eyes.

'That bastard Carver!' A small amount of spittle sprayed from his lips with the outburst. 'Him and his murderous scum.'

Savage looked at Hayes who had a grim expression on his face. Their eyes met and they nodded knowingly at each other.

Savage focused once more on Oliver. 'How many were there?'

Oliver shrugged weary shoulders. 'Forty, fifty. I'm not sure. At the time it seemed like there were a hundred of them. I don't know why so many of us survived.'

Savage patted the man on the shoulder. 'Go and get somethin' to eat, Oliver. My men should have somethin' warm ready by now.'

Savage and Hayes watched him go. A shell of the man he'd formerly been.

'We need to get these bastards, Sir,' Hayes hissed.

'My feelin's exactly, Rube,' Savage acknowledged. 'Find me Private Evans. I want him to ride back to the main column and let the Colonel know what's happened.'

Hayes nodded. 'Right away, Sir.'

'One other thing, Rube,' Savage continued as he looked to the west and noted how low the sun was in the sky. 'We're not stayin'. Give the men a couple of more hours and then we'll head out.'

Hayes nodded his agreement. 'Yes, Sir. Do you want me to send the scouts back out?'

Savage nodded. 'Yes, but make sure they've eaten first.'

After Hayes had left, Savage looked back to the west. The sinking sun had begun to paint a magnificent artwork of long orange streaks through the sky.

Somewhere in the Shenandoah was the killer he'd been tasked to find. He just hoped that it wouldn't be the other way around.

* * *

The column had moved out after dark under the gaze of a silvery moon surrounded by millions of sparkling stars. It was now past midnight and the column made its way along a tree-lined lane, horses hooves echoed in the crisp night air.

'Where do you think they are?' Hayes asked Savage as he broke the silence between them.

He was about to answer when a rider loomed out of the night before them. He dragged back on the horse's reins and it came to a stop across the lane in front of the column. It was Walsh.

'Report, trooper,' Savage said.

'We found 'em, Sir.'

'Where?'

'They're about a mile further up, camped out by a small stream.'

'Pickets?'

'Four or five, Sir.'

Savage looked at Hayes. 'I thought they'd be farther away than this.'

'I guess we just got lucky,' Hayes suggested.

'Or that son of a bitch is so arrogant he doesn't figure on anyone followin' him,' Savage added.

'Don't matter much either way now we've found him.'

Savage thought for a moment as his mount shuffled uneasily beneath him. He turned his attention back to Walsh and asked, 'Is there a way of gettin' around the camp without bein' detected?'

'I think so,' Walsh said hesitantly.

'You've got an hour to make sure,' Savage told him. 'Then get back here.'

'Yes, Sir.'

Walsh whirled his horse about and rode off.

'What's on your mind, Captain?' Hayes asked.

'I figure if we can get around in front of them we can hit them when they move,' Savage explained. 'They won't be expecting us waitin' for them.'

'Why not surround their camp and do it that way?' Hayes pointed out.

'If we did that then we'd have to take care of their pickets,' Savage explained. 'It would only take one mistake doing that and the alarm would be raised and we'd lose all sense of surprise.'

'OK then, I'll have the men move off the lane and into the trees where we'll be out of sight.'

'Have two pickets left here out of sight to watch for Walsh's return.'

★ ★ ★

An hour later, as ordered, Walsh returned with Perry. They'd found a way around and pointed it out on a map spread out by a small fire.

The column was finally in place just before the first light of dawn emerged like fingers over the Blue Ridge Mountains.

Twenty men lay amongst the trees on both sides of the lane under the command of Sergeant-Major Ruben Hayes. The remaining thirty, under the command of Savage, were sequestered farther back in the trees. Once the fighting started, they would split into two groups.

The plan was to hit both front and rear of Carver's column and hopefully cut off any chance of escape.

All they needed now was their quarry.

★ ★ ★

Carver's raiders broke camp shortly
after dawn and continued to travel in
their southerly direction without any
suspicion of what lay in wait for them.
The lane was bordered on both sides by
zigzag rail fences and behind them was
a dense stand of trees.

Carver rode at the head of the column,
ramrod erect in the saddle. There was
another small town to the southwest
and Carver had decided that once they
were finished there they would swing
back up to Kansas and Missouri.

With all of the federal troops filtering
down through the Shenandoah, it was
time to leave.

Carver hipped in the saddle and shouted,
'Sergeant Thomas? To the front.'

Thomas fell in beside Carver. 'What's
up, Sir?'

'Do you feel it?'

Thomas frowned. 'Feel what?'

'Somethin's not right,' Carver said. 'I
can feel it. Pass word back for the men

24

to be ready for anythin'.'

Thomas eased back on the reins of his horse and started to fall back along the column.

At that moment, there was a shout and all hell broke loose as the air became filled with a deadly hailstorm of lead.

⋆　⋆　⋆

On Hayes's order, the hidden Union troops opened up on the raiders. The first volley created a large hole in the line of riders as men and horses went down under the devastating fusillade.

High-pitched squeals of wounded horses filled the early morning air along with cries of panic and confusion. Carver barked orders to his men as a second volley rang out and more men and horses fell.

The hidden Union troops cut the raiders down with methodical preci-sion. A steady rate of fire and reload. It lasted for another two volleys then the raiders gathered themselves and began to return fire at the dismounted cavalry.

Beside Hayes, a trooper cried out and clutched at his face. A river of blood ran between his splayed fingers. He staggered erect in a daze and was immediately knocked back by a second shot.

Farther along the line, more cavalrymen started to scream as Rebel gunfire found its mark. Hayes moved steadily along behind his men giving them encouragement to stay the course heedless of the angry hornets that buzzed about his head.

He paused about two-thirds the way along and dropped to his knee and studied the raiders before him. They had begun to be more organized and it looked as though their leader was preparing to break out of the trap.

'Come on Savage,' he said through gritted teeth. 'Where the hell are you?'

Hayes raised his own Sharps carbine and sighted down the barrel until the foresight rested on Carver. He took a deep breath and slowly let it out.

'Take this you son of a bitch,' he cursed and gently squeezed the trigger.

Something hard punched into the Sergeant-Major's left shoulder which threw off his aim at the precise moment the Sharps discharged its .54 caliber round. The shot flew high and wide and missed its intended target by quite a distance.

Hayes cursed out loud. Not from the pain that burned in his shoulder but from the fact he'd missed Carver. Beside him, another toppled sideways with a bullet to his chest.

The Sergeant-Major discarded the Sharps and drew his sidearm. He could feel blood start to run down the arm that dangled uselessly at his side.

Ignoring the pain, he sighted on a raider and squeezed the trigger. Hayes's target was obscured momentarily by a great plume of gun smoke discharged from the end of his barrel but when it cleared, the only thing he saw was the riderless horse.

Through the sound of gunfire, he heard the brassy sound of a bugle. He sighed with relief. 'About bloody time.'

The two groups of cavalry came thundering along the lane from both directions, sabers drawn and screaming bloody murder.

Savage was out in front of the first group, bearing down on the head of the raider column. He held his saber out at arm's length, cutting edge facing upwards. The two groups hit with an audible thump as the galloping Union cavalry drove into the ranks of raiders.

Just as his horse was about to make contact with another mount, Savage brought his saber down and right in a backhanded slash that cleaved open a raider's chest, blood sprayed from the wound.

The melee was bloody and frantic. At close quarters it was sabers against six-guns and the raiders had expended valuable ammunition in the first furious moments of battle. Now hammers began to fall on empty chambers.

Savage swung at a rider pointing a six-gun in his direction. The cavalry blade sheared through flesh and bone and the pistol, complete with a hand attached, dropped to the churned up earth beneath the raider's horse.

The man held his stump up in bewilderment, eyes wide as he stared at the blood spurting from the deadly wound. Savage swung the blade again and opened the man's throat.

All around him, men fought desperately and as Savage swung his horse about to locate another target, he came face to face with a raider's .36 caliber Navy Colt.

Time froze while Savage stared into the black hole of the gun's barrel. He saw the finger tighten on the trigger and the hammer fall.

Nothing happened. The Colt was empty.

Suddenly, one side of the raider's head exploded outwards spraying blood, bone, and flesh into the air.

Savage swung about to see Hayes

standing with his Colt still level at shoulder height surrounded by a cloud of blue-gray gun smoke. The remaining men with him had emerged from cover and were closing in on the raiders.

Loud shouting from Savage's left attracted his attention. He turned his horse and saw the man who wore Confederate pants and the coat of a Union Major.

'Carver!' Savage shouted, not realizing he'd done so until the killer swung to look in his direction.

He smiled wickedly as though reveling in the blood and carnage of battle.

Savage kicked his mount hard to drive it towards him.

Carver, still smiling, raised his own pistol and aimed at Savage.

Savage saw the gesture and raised his saber ready for the killing blow. The horse buffeted its way through the scrimmage towards where Carver sat atop his mount. He saw the killer's thumb ratchet the hammer back and he knew that nothing would save him this time.

There was a puff of gun smoke and

Savage felt the bullet strike him hard in the chest. The slug buried deep and a moment of numbness spread over his body.

When the pain came, it was deep and burning. It washed over Savage in a wave which caused him to clench his jaw firm and hunch over in the saddle. He looked up and saw Carver smiling at him.

All around, the battle continued to rage, and the sound echoed hollowly in Savage's ears. He could feel his strength ebbing fast and grabbed for the pommel of his saddle to prevent the fall he knew was imminent.

His horse lurched to the side and Savage missed it completely. He began to fall towards the ground and an all-consuming blackness.

3

Texas, spring 1866.

Ten men rode past the battered sign that read Summerton just after noon on a bright sunny day. They were dressed in rags that were left over from the civil war.

The day was warm without being hot and the riders seemed to sit comfortably in the saddle. Every single one of them wore the stamp of an outlaw.

These were the last remnants of Carver's raiders, plus a few extras they'd picked up along the way. Now they had come to Texas.

John Carver rode at their head. Gone was the Major's jacket he had worn during their raid in the Shenandoah Valley. It had been replaced by a plain brown coat. About his waist, he wore a dual holster gun belt which housed two

Colt army model six-guns. Tucked away in a shoulder holster he had a .36 caliber pocket Navy revolver.

Behind Carver rode Ringo Thomas, a man who'd been by Carver's side when they'd been bushwhacked in the Shenandoah. Out of the forty-three men, Carver had had with him that day, only five extricated themselves from the killing field.

They were Carver, Ringo Thomas, Simon Cooper, Clint Ross, and Buster Jarvis. The others, Duane Brooks, Anderson White, Chase Hunter, Cody, and Donnie Gardener had all joined later.

The last five men were a ragtag jumble of deserters.

After the war, they'd continued their outlaw ways, and robbed and murdered their way through the northern states. When it became too hot for them, Carver decided to head for Texas. They rode into Summerton for one last job before going their separate ways.

Surrounded by hills of limestone and granite rocks, the town of Summerton sat on a small expanse of green. A small spring-fed stream ran to the east of the town and the foothills were covered in cedar scrub.

Summerton's population numbered around seven hundred and the Summerton Savings and Loan held all of their money.

As the outlaws rode along the false-fronted main street in twin columns, the horses hooves kicked up small clouds of dust from the dry earth.

Every person who saw the group ride past stopped and stared then lowered their gaze and hurried on. There was something about the men that spelled trouble.

They rode on past the livery and the blacksmith's shop without hesitation. Further along, they passed the Longhorn saloon and the Summerton hotel.

Carver gave the sheriff's office a cursory glance as they passed it then turned his gaze back to the street. Behind him, the last four men of the column dropped out and took up position across the street from the jail. Six men continued forward until they found what they were looking for.

The Summerton Savings and Loan was a false-fronted building with two large windows and a central door. The sign atop the veranda awning was painted in bold green letters.

Carver and the five men with him turned their mounts towards the hitching rail out front and eased them to a stop.

They looped the reins over the cross beam and climbed onto the boardwalk.

'Hunter, Ross, wait here,' Carver snapped. 'Keep an eye on the horses.'

Without another word, Carver and the other three entered the bank.

⋆ ⋆ ⋆

Cletus Stewart, the manager of the Summerton Savings and Loan, looked up when the outlaws entered and frowned. He was curious about the four scruffy men and what they could want with his bank?

As he stared at one man, a solidly-built man with blond hair and blue eyes, he felt a sense of foreboding build within him.

The bank's other customers didn't take much notice of the four men who had entered the bank. Two were women and the other was a man named Calvin.

One lady, dressed in a pale-blue dress, was being served by Floyd Walker, the bank teller. The other woman was being served by Stewart while the well-dressed Calvin waited patiently for his turn.

It wasn't until Carver drew one of his Colts and crossed swiftly to the counter that they became aware that things inside the bank were about to go awfully wrong.

He stuck the six-gun under the manager's nose and snarled, 'I'd like to make a withdrawal.'

The two ladies gasped with shock at the sight of the gun pressed to Stewart's face. Instinctively, Calvin moved to back away and came up hard against the six-gun of Ringo Thomas.

'Goin' somewhere?' the brown haired man whispered harshly.

Calvin froze instantly and his hands shot skyward.

'Cody,' Carver snapped, 'Get around there and empty that there safe.'

The safe was a large MacNeale and Urban construction and when Cody tried to open it, the door stayed fast.

'It's locked,' he called across to Carver.

Carver applied pressure to his Colt and spoke into the manager's ear, his voice full of menace. 'Open it. And don't try anythin' fancy or I'll plug you.'

Cody walked up behind a wide-eyed Stewart and grabbed him by the collar. He dragged him towards the safe and held his gun on him while the man fumbled with the safe, his hands trembling with terror.

Meanwhile, the women stood and cowered together in a corner next to Calvin while the fourth outlaw, Duane Brooks, stood guard on them.

Carver watched as the safe's heavy door swung open to reveal stacks of notes and sacks of coins. He smiled mirthlessly and said, 'Hurry up and empty out one of them sacks and stuff the notes into it.'

Cody shoved Stewart out of the way hard enough to make him stagger. He grabbed a sack of coins and emptied it onto the floor noisily. Fistfuls of notes soon refilled the empty money sack.

Carver watched on greedily. He was so intent on making sure that Cody got all of the paper money from the safe that he had a momentary lapse in concentration and forgot about Walker the teller.

Using the distraction, Walker slipped his hand under the counter and grasped the butt of the old Colt Dragoon that was hidden there.

The teller's intentions became abundantly clear with the loud triple-click of the hammer ratcheting back. Carver snapped his gaze to Walker in time to see the gun barrel rise up from behind the desk.

Carver reacted with speed and precision to the threat and swung his Colt and squeezed the trigger. The six-gun roared and the slug punched through the teller's chest and out his back, spraying crimson across the room.

Ringo Thomas whirled from the window at the sound of the shot.

'What the hell?' he shouted in time to see Carver shift his aim and point his smoking Colt at Stewart.

The bank manager threw his hands up as high as he could and screamed, 'Don't shoot! I didn't do anything.'

'You should have,' Carver snarled and pulled the trigger.

Thunder filled the room once more and the bank manager's head snapped back with a neat hole in his forehead. More blood sprayed, this time over Cody who was behind him shoving the last of the money into the sack.

'I guess we need to be goin', Major,' Thomas suggested.

'When I'm ready,' Carver snapped.

'I'm done, Major,' Cody said and stood up.

'There's people startin' to gather

outside,' Thomas warned. 'They've got guns.'

Carver nodded and looked at the three trembling forms in the corner.

'Brooks, shoot the feller and bring the women with us,' Carver ordered. 'Maybe them townsfolk might think twice about shootin' at us with them along.'

'Wait. No!' Calvin protested fearfully, holding out his hands in a feeble attempt to prevent the inevitable. 'Please don't.'

Brooks shrugged nonchalantly and squeezed the trigger. Calvin died with a pleading and fearful look on his face and his body slumped to the floor.

Both women screamed as they were grabbed roughly and propelled towards the door by Thomas and Brooks.

The following events occurred with such ferocity that they would be talked about for years to come.

★ ★ ★

Sheriff Matt Bryson and his deputy, Billy Peters had just entered the jail from the rear when an old timer named Ira blundered through the front door.

Bryson had been sheriff of Summerton for the past six years and although now past the age of forty-five, could still perform his duties adequately to keep the town council happy.

His deputy was half his age and where Bryson was solid, Peters was gangly.

They had been talking when Ira burst in but the old man's face brought about an abrupt halt to their conversation.

'What's up Ira?' Bryson asked. 'You look like you've seen a ghost or somethin'.'

'He's here,' the pale-faced old timer gasped. 'I saw him with my own eyes. Rode into town as large as life.'

Bryson frowned. 'Who's here?'

Ira's eyes widened. 'John Carver.'

Billy Peters chuckled. 'Have you been drinkin', old man?'

'No, Sir. He's here alright,' Ira confirmed. 'He even left some men across the street. They're just sittin' there watchin' the jail.'

'How do you know it's him?' Peters asked sceptically.

'I seen him before the war. He passed through here once. I'd know his face anywhere.'

Bryson walked over to the window and looked across the street and confirmed what Ira had said. Four men, sitting, watching, waiting for something.

The lawman thought for a moment then crossed to the gun-rack that hung on the wall near a blackened potbellied stove. He took down a coach gun and a Henry rifle.

The latter he tossed across to Peters.

The deputy looked questioningly at Bryson and the sheriff nodded. 'He was right. There's four strangers across the street watchin' the jail.'

Bryson crossed to his scarred desk and opened a drawer. From it, he dug out some shotgun shells loaded two into the breech of the coach gun then stuffed some spares into his pockets.

Next, he found a box of cartridges for the Henry and gave them to Peters. He gave the young man a serious look and said, 'When the shootin' starts, keep your head down and don't do anythin' stupid. These fellers are killers and they won't hesitate to shoot.'

Peters felt his nerves start to jangle and he began to feel queasy. He nodded jerkily. 'OK, sure.'

Bryson turned his steely gaze on Ira. 'Can you go out the back door and round up some help?'

The old timer swallowed then cleared his throat. 'I can do that. I think.'

'Get Ed, George, Ben, Grayson, Walter, and anyone else you can think of who can shoot,' Bryson ordered.

After Ira left, Bryson turned to Peters and said, 'Are you ready?'

He nodded uncertainly.

'Let's go.'

'Wait,' Peters blurted out. 'You ain't goin' out the front are you?'

'I ain't walkin' out into that, Billy,' Bryson assured his deputy. 'I ain't gotten to this age by doin' foolish things. We'll head out the back and come up the alleyway. There's more cover there. Once we get into position, I'm hoping to have some more help.'

They exited the jail and circled left and made their way up the alley when the thunder of shots sounded from the bank.

'Hell and damnation,' Bryson cursed. 'Follow me and don't stop. Keep movin' and firin'.'

When they burst from the mouth of the alley, the outlaws who'd staked out the jail were already mounted and now spurred their mounts along the street.

Bryson propped and unloaded a double charge of buckshot after them but the riders showed no effects from the deadly hail of pellets.

Meanwhile, Billy fired the Henry, levered and fired again. Bryson noticed a rider lurch in his saddle after the second shot but remain mounted.

'Come on, Billy,' Bryson called to his deputy and started to jog along the street.

From a distance, Bryson could see a commotion out the front of the bank. Small puffs of gun smoke bloomed and the flat reports of six-guns cracked out as townsmen engaged the outlaws in a gun battle. He saw two women struggle as they were dragged from the bank and forced up onto waiting horses.

The two lawmen quickened their pace and as they neared the bank, all of the outlaws were mounted.

The intensity of the gunfire had increased and Bryson knew that it would be a miracle if the women came through their predicament unscathed.

He stopped in the center of the street and shouted above the pandemonium, 'Watch the women you fools! Aim for the horses.'

Bryson watched in horror as he saw a bright red stain appear on the front of one woman's dress. The outlaw who had hold of her, released her limp form and she slid silently to the street.

Stunned and transfixed by what he had just witnessed, Bryson failed to see the outlaw train his gun in his direction. When the hammer fell, the six-gun roared and Bryson felt the slug slam into his chest. He staggered drunkenly, in an attempt to remain upright. He stared down at his bloody chest then back at the outlaw who'd fired at him. The killer was ready to take his second shot.

Bryson moved like molasses as he made a try for his own sidearm but was dead before his hand even touched it. The second bullet from the outlaw's gun smashed into his chest and his world went black.

'No!' Peters screamed loudly and swung up the Henry. He snapped off a shot and saw the killer throw up his arms then fall from the saddle. Peters took cover beside a water trough as bullets drummed a tattoo on its hardened exterior.

Another rider with a bullet in the right side of his chest fell from his horse but fired wildly into the mêlée.

Out of the corner of his eye, Peters

saw a townsman get hit, stumble, and fall. Then another took a slug.

With the sheriff dead, Peters knew that he was the one the townsfolk would look to for leadership. Without further thought, he stood up and walked out into the street.

He began to fire the Henry, levered and fired, levered and fired. When a hammering blow struck him in his right side, Peters went down on one knee and pressed a hand to his wound. When he took it away he saw the wet redness of his blood.

He gritted his teeth and stood once more but quickly took another slug. It hit Peters in the left leg above the knee which caused him to crash onto the street. Pain shot through his body and into his brain. He screamed shrilly and lost his grip on the rifle.

There was more shouting and then the gunfire dwindled away to nothing. As he lay there, pain caused the world to spin before his eyes. He heard voices that seemed distant and indistinct.

One of them said with alarm, 'The sheriff is dead.'

Another said bitterly, 'So is Mary.'

'Who was the woman they took?'

Peters thought that voice sounded like Burns from the livery stable.

As he was on the verge of an all-consuming blackness, he heard, 'It was Amy. The bastards took Amy Savage.'

4

'Hold it there, Blue-belly,' a voice drawled from the thick brush at the side of the road.

Savage drew back on the reins and brought his bay mare to a stop in the bright morning sunshine. He was two days from home and he hadn't survived years of war to die now.

He still wore his union blue cavalry pants and the shirt to match. He'd swapped his captain's coat for a buckskin jacket on his trip south but his boots still had some life in them. His Hardee was gone and had been replaced by a low-crowned hat.

'Keep your hands up and away from that six-gun you got holstered there,' the voice spoke again.

Savage raised his hands to shoulder height. 'Now what?'

'You can come on out Jeb,' the voice called.

From the left and rear of Savage sprang a tall, string-bean looking man dressed in Confederate rags. In his hands was a Spencer carbine.

With a rustle to his front, the speaker emerged. He was dressed in a similar fashion to his accomplice, though he was a little shorter. He too was armed with a Spencer.

The man smiled, a disgusting black-toothed smile and said, 'Well lookee what we got here, Jeb.'

Savage followed the man's gaze to the Winchester rifle in his saddle scabbard. The man stepped forward and placed his hand on the rifle's stock. He was about to take it out when Savage's right hand locked on his wrist in a vice-like grip.

The man looked at Savage, pain evident in his eyes.

'You let me go, Yank, or Jeb there will shoot you full of holes,' he warned.

'Who the hell are you?' Savage demanded.

The man ignored the question and

slid the Winchester out of the scabbard. He whistled appreciatively at the gun they called the 'Yellow Boy' with the octagonal barrel. It was basically an improvement of the design of the Henry and fired the .44 Henry cartridge.

'That sure is a mighty fine rifle, yes sir, mighty fine,' he turned to his friend. 'Look Jeb. Did you ever see such a fine rifle in all your born days?'

'No,' the answer was long and drawn out.

'I asked you who you were?' Savage said patiently.

The man looked at Savage sideways and his expression changed from one of appreciation for the rifle to one of disdain for the man.

He spat on the ground and when he spoke, his voice was full of scorn. 'Alright Blue-belly, I'll answer your question. My name is Lucius. You already know Jeb's name. Now, who are you?'

'Jeff Savage.'

'And where might you be goin', Savage?'

'Summerton.'

'You got some land there you figure on stealin' from a hard workin' Texas boy?'

'I'm goin' home,' Savage told him.

Lucius was surprised. 'You a son of Texas?'

'Yeah.'

Lucius screwed his face up and pointed the Winchester at Savage.

'What you are is a traitor,' he snarled. 'And do you know what we do with scum like you? We hang 'em.'

Savage tensed.

'Now get the hell off that horse.'

Savage eased down from the saddle. 'You're makin' a mistake friend.'

'The only mistake around here was made by you, oh and I ain't yer friend,' Lucius snapped back at him. 'Figgerin' you could come back to Texas. Get a rope Jeb.'

'We ain't got a rope, Lucius,' Jeb drawled slowly.

'I knew that. Shut up,' Lucius bawled. 'We'll just damn well shoot him instead. And we'll use his own rifle to do it with.'

As he brought the rifle up to fire, Lucius made a couple of errors in judgment. The first was the failure to take the Remington .44 caliber six-gun from Savage's holster. The second was not checking to see that there was a load in the Winchester's breech.

If he had taken the time, he would've known that there was nothing under the hammer.

There was a dry click when the hammer fell on an empty chamber and Lucius' eyebrows raised in surprise. His look changed to one of fear as he desperately worked the Winchester's lever.

'I told you, you were makin' a mistake,' Savage said and drew the Remington.

The gun thundered and the slug blew a hole in Lucius' skull, killing him instantly. Savage swiveled at the hips and snapped off a shot that struck Jeb in the chest before he could fire his Spencer.

The tall man fell back and sat down hard. Stunned, he sat blinking, a red stain steadily growing across his chest. He looked up at Savage, confused.

Jeb opened his mouth to speak but nothing came out. Then his eyes rolled up and he slumped backwards, dead.

Savage checked both men before he retrieved their weapons and threw them in the brush. He picked up his Winchester, put it back in its scabbard and reloaded his Remington.

He ran his gaze over the fateful two and shook his head. For a fleeting moment, he considered burying them but then it was gone. Murderers like them didn't deserve a decent burial.

Savage turned his back on them, caught up the reins of his bay and climbed aboard. Without a backward glance, he rode off. He was going home and nothing was about to stop him.

The sky overhead was a clear blue and the sun had drenched the landscape with its warmth when Savage rode into Summerton's deserted main street just before noon on the second day.

As he rode, he pondered his wife's reaction when she finally saw him. How would she have changed? How much had he changed? And changed he had, just as the war had changed so many.

Savage frowned and drew the bay to a stop. Where was everyone? The street looked to be uninhabited.

'Jeff Savage? Is that you?' a voice called out.

Savage turned his attention to a man who'd emerged from an alley between the Longhorn saloon and the Summerton hotel.

'Ira?'

Ira rushed over to where Savage had stopped his horse.

Savage climbed down to greet the man and they shook firmly.

55

'Damn, Savage, it is you. Man am I sure glad to see you,' Ira beamed. 'Word was you were dead. But Miss Amy wouldn't believe it. No, sir.'

Savage smiled. 'Well, at least it wasn't loaded guns that met me as I rode in. It's good to see you, Ira. How've you been?'

Savage noticed a sudden change come over his face.

'Where is everyone?' he asked looking about.

'They're at the funerals,' Ira answered somberly.

'What funerals? Who died?'

'Sheriff Bryson, Floyd Walker the bank manager, and Cletus Stewart the teller,' Ira explained. 'They buried Mary, Calvin, and Ben Hamilton yesterday.'

'What happened?' Savage asked concerned at the extent of the death toll.

'John Carver,' Ira told him bitterly. 'That's what happened.'

Savage felt a chill run down his spine and rubbed absently at his chest.

'The murderin' son of a bitch and his

gang robbed the Savings and Loan three days ago,' Ira continued. 'There was a terrible ruckus and when it was all over, they was all dead. Bryson's deputy was wounded along with two others. They're all over at Doc Handley's place.'

'What about Carver?'

'Bastard got away,' Ira said with disgust. 'But we brought down two of them, though. Killed one man and the other feller is only wounded. Got him locked away in the jail.'

'Who led the posse if the town was down two lawmen?' Savage inquired.

Ira shook his head. 'Nobody. They just let 'em get away with all of the town's money. Not one man in Summerton was willin' to put their hand up to go after 'em.'

'Don't be too harsh on 'em, Ira,' Savage soothed. 'Carver and his men are a bad bunch.'

Ira looked him in the eye and Savage couldn't help but feel the old timer had held something back.

'Is there somethin' you ain't tellin' me, Ira?' he asked.

'Aww hell, Jeff . . . ' Ira started.

'Tell me.'

'When they left, they weren't alone, Jeff,' Ira began to explain hesitantly. 'When they robbed the bank, Amy was there too. They took her with 'em. I'm sorry.'

Savage felt as though he'd been punched in the middle and been robbed of the air from his lungs. His world spun as a million unanswered questions entered his head. He gathered himself and his icy gaze settled back on Ira. 'Which way did they go?'

'It was three days ago, Jeff,' Ira reasoned. 'They're long gone. It has even rained since then. Any tracks will be washed out.'

All Savage could think about was Amy and the man who had taken her.

'Which way?' Savage grated.

'South,' Ira informed him. 'But listen, wait for me. I'll get a horse and come with you. Maybe I can help.'

But Savage waited for no one. He leaped back onto the mare and swung her head around.

'Wait, Jeff,' Ira protested again, as he made a grab for the horse's bridle. 'Let me help.'

'You and the town have helped enough,' he snarled. 'Now get the hell out of my way.'

Savage heeled the bay savagely and brought it quickly to full stride. As he left town, Savage passed the large crowd gathered at the Summerton cemetery. The strains of 'Rock of Ages' hung over them like a heavy cloud.

★　★　★

Savage found his wife five miles from Summerton in a stand of trees. He would have missed her as he rode on blindly, except he caught sight of a vulture waddling on the ground. Then another and yet another.

He eased the horse down to a walk and pointed it towards the ugly looking black birds. Once off the trail, he dismounted and took a number of lurching steps.

Savage walked onward, an invisible hand pushing him unwittingly forward. From deep within, his dread began to rise. Something told him to stop but he knew that he had to see, needed to know.

In a small patch of clear ground, he saw Amy's white, naked body in stark contrast against the black of the huddled vultures.

The Remington roared twice before Savage realized that it was in his hand. The sickening carrion eaters took flight and he could now see the body more clearly.

He took a few more paces forward then fell to his knees. He looked to the heavens and screamed, 'No!'

The pain he felt in his chest was entirely different to the bullet he'd taken in '64. This felt like he was being torn apart.

He stared at the body of his wife

once more then leaned forward and emptied the contents of his stomach onto the ground.

* * *

Amy Savage was buried three days later, beneath a cloudless sky in the Summerton cemetery. It was a small service. Though Amy had been well liked in the community, it was apparent that there was a certain element in Summerton unable or unprepared to forget that her husband had been a federal cavalry captain. Even Amy's parents had felt the same way but the need to farewell to their only daughter had been stronger and they couldn't stay away.

After the service, Savage saddled his horse and bought supplies from the grocer. Once finished there, he walked along to the gunsmith's shop where he bought ammunition for the Winchester and the Remington He also purchased another Remington six-gun which he wrapped in an oilskin cloth and placed in his saddlebags.

Savage was about to climb into the saddle when Ira showed.

'Are you leavin'?' he asked.

Savage said nothing.

'You're goin' after them ain't you?'

'What do you think?' Savage snapped. 'They killed my wife and it's my fault.'

'How do you figure that Son?' Ira asked. 'You weren't even here. There was nothin' you could have done.'

'Not true,' Savage said. 'Back in '64 we were in the Shenandoah and so was Carver. I was tasked with stoppin' him and his raiders. We caught up with 'em and set up an ambush. We wiped out most of them except for a handful. And Carver was one of them. Son of a bitch put a bullet in me and got away. So you see, it is my fault.'

'You can't blame yourself for what happened in the war.'

'Well, I aim to make amends for it,' Savage assured the old timer. 'I'll hunt him down and make him pay. You just wait and see.'

'But you don't even know where they were headed,' Ira pointed out.

Savage thought for a moment then nodded. 'You're right. But I know someone who does.'

'What? Who?'

But Savage had already turned and was walking towards the jail, leading his horse.

When he entered he found the young deputy, Billy Peters, sitting behind the desk. He was still recovering from his wounds but was determined to continue in a limited capacity and not overdo it. The town had hired someone to help out while he was laid up.

Peters stood up slowly when Savage walked through the door and greeted him. 'Mr. Savage, how can I help?'

'I want to talk to your prisoner,' Savage told him.

Peters hesitated then said, 'I don't think that is a good idea.'

'I ain't askin', I'm tellin'. I'm goin' to talk to your prisoner.'

Savage crossed to the rear of the

room and the door through to the cells. He paused and removed a key from a hook beside the door then kept going.

'Wait,' Peters protested. 'You can't go back there.'

Ira and the deputy followed Savage through in time to see him open the door of the cell.

The outlaw looked at him curiously. 'What do you want?'

'What's your name?' Savage asked.

The man stood up favoring his right shoulder and side. 'What's it to you?'

The fact that the man was injured had not gone unnoticed by Savage and his left fist shot out and hit the man a solid blow in the wounded region.

The outlaw screamed and staggered back.

'Hey,' Peters' voice rose incredulously. 'You can't . . . '

He never finished because Savage had drawn his Remington which was now pointed at the young man.

'Shut down,' Savage hissed. 'This feller and his friends were responsible for the death of my wife. So I will deal with him as I see fit.'

Peters paled noticeably but remained silent.

'Take it easy, Savage,' Ira cautioned.

Savage turned back to the ashen-faced outlaw and placed the muzzle of the six-gun against his left thigh.

'Now, what is your name?'

'Donnie Gardener,' he gasped out.

Savage nodded. 'Where is Carver headed?'

Gardener smiled coldly. 'I don't know.'

The Remington crashed and the outlaw fell to the cell floor, grasping his leg and screaming loudly.

'What the hell?' shouted Peters who made to step forward.

Savage whirled about and slammed the cell door shut. He reached through the bars and turned the key so the door locked. Then he took the key from the lock and stuffed it into his pocket.

'Open the door, Savage.' Peters snapped.

Savage ignored him and returned to

where Gardener lay clutching his bloody leg. This time, he placed the gun against the man's head. 'Let's try again. Where is Carver goin'?'

'Son of a bitch, I don't know,' he hissed through the pain.

The Remington's hammer ratcheted back.

'No wait!' he cried out. 'I told you I don't know. They were goin' to split up.'

'You must know somethin'? Talk.'

After a few seconds of silence, Savage pressed the cold barrel of the six-gun harder against his head. 'Wait! Buckley. Ross said somethin' about goin' to Buckley.'

'What else?'

'That's it, honest.'

'What about names?' Savage said. 'Give me names.'

Without hesitation, Gardener told Savage the names of the other outlaws.

Satisfied, he let down the hammer on the Remington and holstered it. He unlocked the door and opened it to leave.

There was a murmur from Gardener

and Savage turned and locked him in an icy stare. 'What did you say?'

'I said I bet they had some fun with her before they killed her.'

Savage stared at the sinister smile on the outlaw's face and without even a blink, drew the Remington once more and shot the gloating Gardener between the eyes.

As the echo of the shot died away the two stunned men who'd been witnesses remained silent. Savage holstered his gun and brushed past them as he exited. He walked through the open door and out into the office.

Without stopping, he made for the front door and had just opened it when Peters stopped him.

'Hold it, Savage,' he ordered, his voice full of authority. 'I'm arrestin' you for murder.'

Savage gave him a withering glare and said, 'You what?'

'I'm arrestin' you. You can't just shoot a man like that and expect to walk out of here.'

Savage snorted derisively. 'Go and play sheriff somewhere else kid. I'm leavin' and you ain't goin' to stop me. Besides, somebody has to show some spine and stop Carver.'

Peters wanted to go on with it but the doorway was empty. He hurried across to the chair at the desk, took out his six-gun from its holster and followed Savage out the door.

Savage was climbing into the saddle and Peters thumbed back the hammer and aimed it.

'I told you to stop, Savage,' he shouted.

Townsfolk stopped to stare at the spectacle playing out before them. A murmur ran through the onlookers.

Savage ignored him and turned the horse away and started to ride off.

The gun hammer went back to full cock. 'I said stop!'

A calloused hand reached out and pushed the barrel of the gun down.

'Let him go, Son,' Ira said softly. 'He deserves his chance at Carver. He'll find him.'

Peters nodded, gave Savage one last glance, turned around and walked back inside.

'And God help him when he does,' Ira murmured.

5

Clementine slipped quietly out of bed and padded across the room. Through the window, the moonlight cast a silvery glow which gave her white skin luminosity.

Somewhere in the town, a dog barked at an unseen disturbance.

The man in her bed snuffled, snorted, and settled. She cast a nervous glance over her shoulder. This wasn't the first time she'd riffled a client's pockets. And if he woke up, it wouldn't be the first time she'd been caught.

Clint Ross coughed, rolled over on the lumpy mattress and settled once more.

Clementine picked up the outlaw's pants and started going through his pockets. The left one contained a few coins and the right was much of the same.

She dropped the trousers and grabbed Ross' jacket. She found what she was looking for in his right pocket. A large roll of paper money. She took it out and smiled broadly and the moonlight glinted off her even teeth.

'What the hell do you think you're doin'?' Ross snarled.

Clementine jumped and dropped the money.

'I . . . I . . . ,' she stammered. 'Nothin'. I wasn't doin' nothin'.'

Ross climbed out of bed in his underwear and stood up. Even though he was a shade under six-feet tall, at that moment, to Clementine he looked unnaturally tall.

'Lyin' bitch,' he spat. 'You were tryin' to rob me.'

Clementine backed up, shaking her head vigorously. 'No. No, I wasn't. Honest.'

But Ross was beyond reason and he advanced on her with his six-gun in his fist. He had blood in his eye and was determined to teach Clementine a lesson.

Before he reached her, the screams

started and filled the top floor of the Golden Garter saloon.

⋆ ⋆ ⋆

The proprietor of the Golden Garter, Ernie West was ripped violently from his slumber by piercing shrieks from along the hall. He rolled from his bed and shook off the vestiges of sleep that dulled his brain.

He scooped up a small .36 caliber pocket Navy revolver and charged from his room into the lamp-lit hall. Already a group of working girls had gathered outside their rooms and one, a buxom girl named Lilly, rushed up to him.

'He's killin' her,' she blurted out. 'He's killin' Clementine. You gotta do somethin'.'

'The stupid bitch was probably tryin' to roll him,' another girl snorted. 'She's probably gettin' what she deserves.'

'Shut up Esther,' Lilly snapped and turned her attention back to West. 'Do somethin'.'

The crash of breaking furniture and more screams spurred West into action. He charged along the hallway to Clementine's room. He tried the knob but the door was locked. He took a step back and brought his bare foot up and drove it hard against the door.

The jamb splintered with a dry crack and the door crashed back revealing Ross standing over Clementine where she cowered in the far corner of the room.

West stepped into the doorway and leveled his gun. 'Hey! Stop that.'

Ross whirled, brought up his own gun and squeezed the trigger. The small room rocked with the fiery discharge and the slug hit the saloon owner dead center. The impact threw him backward across the hall where he crashed against the wall, and slid to the floor, leaving a bloody trail that shone in the lamplight.

Lilly rushed forward and knelt beside her dead boss. She looked around futilely.

'Somebody help us!' she screamed.

That was when the unshaven stranger, wearing only blue cavalry pants and carrying a .44 Remington, appeared.

It was after dark when Savage had ridden his weary bay into Buckley. He'd been on the trail, riding hard for five days and both he and his horse were about done in. He'd put up the mare at the livery and find a meal and bed for the night. If the man he was looking for was here, he'd still be here first thing in the morning.

The evening was cool and cloudless. Above the town, a large moon hung in a web of winking stars. The main street was lit by intermittently spaced lamplight.

Savage rode past the false-fronted sheriff's office and tucked its location away in his mind for the morning. He also made out the local gunsmith, general store, bank, telegraph office, hotel, and the Golden Garter. The latter was a bevy of activity.

He was starting to think he may have missed the livery when it loomed up on his left on the far side of town.

It was a large barn-style affair with double doors. The doors were still open and a kerosene lantern hung on a nail driven into an upright post.

Savage dismounted and led the bay inside.

'Hello?' he called out.

A balding man in his forties stuck his head around the corner of a stall and said, 'Be right with you stranger.'

When the man reappeared he said, 'Sorry about that, I got a horse back there is gettin' ready to foal. Now, what can I do for you?'

'Need a stall for the night.'

The livery man nodded. 'Sure, I can do that Mr . . . ?'

'Savage.'

'Sure, Mr. Savage. I'm Henley by the way,' he said introducing himself. 'It'll cost you four bits for the stall.'

'What about feed?' Savage asked.

'All included.'

After the mare was settled into a clean stall, Savage looked at Henley and asked, 'Are there any strangers in town? Maybe come in over the past few days?'

Henley studied him carefully. 'You lookin' for anyone in particular?'

'Feller called Ross.'

Henley thought for a moment then shook his head. 'Nope, name don't ring a bell. Friend of yours?'

'Not hardly.'

Savage scooped up the Winchester and his saddlebags and turned to walk away when Henley stopped him.

'Mind you,' he said, 'I don't get every stranger's name who comes in. I know of four strangers in town but not all of 'em gave me a name. Add to that I only do evenin's here so if they came in through the day then I wouldn't see 'em. You might try sheriff Miller, though, he's usually on top of these things.'

'Obliged,' said Savage and kept walking.

* * *

Savage pushed through the door at the hotel and walked across uneven floor-boards to the counter. He picked up a small bell from the polished counter top and gave it a sharp ring.

A bleary-eyed man came from a small back room and Savage guessed that he'd interrupted the man's evening nap.

'Can I get a room?' Savage inquired.

The clerk looked at him and gave an apologetic smile. 'Sorry stranger but we're full up.'

Savage gave the clerk a suspicious look which made the man a little nervous and he shuffled his feet.

'Do you know where I might find somethin' else?'

'The Golden Garter might have something, Sir,' he suggested.

Even though he was dubious about it all, Savage surmised that it would be better than nothing. Without another word he turned and left.

Once outside, he followed the board-walk until he found the suggested establishment. The noise that greeted Savage made him think twice before entering.

He shook his head then walked through the doors and into a smoke-filled room with dull light cast from lamps hanging on rough plank walls.

As Savage bellied-up to the bar, a bearded barkeep came down to greet him. 'What'll it be, stranger?'

'Whiskey.'

The barkeep nodded and moved along the bar to find an open bottle. While the man was gone, Savage looked around the room. Most of the tables were occupied. Some men played cards while others bought drinks for the ladies who laughed gaily.

A man caught his eye and gave him an unhappy look. Then Savage remembered that he still wore cavalry pants. And at this time in Texas, it would be a sore point indeed.

When the barkeep walked back, he reached below the scarred counter and grabbed a shot-glass. He popped the cork and slopped the amber liquid into the glass then corked the bottle.

Putting some change on the bar, Savage asked, 'Have you got a room for the night?'

'All the rooms are for the girls,' he was informed.

Savage put up some more money and the barkeep stared at him for a time before he said, 'I reckon we might be able to find you somethin'. The name is Ernie West, I own the saloon.'

'Jeff Savage,' he said, offering his name.

'What brings you to Buckley?' West asked.

'I'm lookin' for someone,' Savage informed him. 'Goes by the name of Clint Ross. Heard the name mentioned lately?'

West nodded. 'Sure.'

A surge of anticipation buzzed within Savage and he asked, 'Do you know where I might find him?'

'Honestly, I have no idea,' West answered. 'I haven't seen him since early on. But he won't have gone far.'

'Why's that?' Savage asked, in an

attempt to conceal his disappointment.

'He's got a good roll of money on him,' West elaborated. 'In my experience, he won't be leavin' town until it's all gone.'

'Is that it?'

'Well, that and the fact he's got a friend here.'

The feeling came back. 'Where?'

West just shrugged.

'You don't know?'

'Don't worry, Savage. If they come in here tomorrow, I'll let 'em know you're lookin' for them.'

'No!' Savage snapped. 'Don't tell 'em anythin'.'

West frowned. 'Why not?'

After tossing back the drink, Savage said pragmatically, 'Because if Ross is who I think he is, I aim to kill him.'

★ ★ ★

The room was small and smelled musty. Savage moved over to the window and opened it a fraction to let in some fresh air.

The mattress on the iron-framed bed was lumpy but that didn't worry Savage. He removed his shirt to reveal a well sculpted, if somewhat hairy torso with a purple, puckered bullet scar on his chest.

The cavalry boots went in the corner beneath a rickety chair and the gun belt with the Remington was looped over the bed post.

Before he lay down, Savage took the saddlebags from his bed and dumped them on the chair then leaned the Winchester against it too.

The effects of the whiskey and days of hard travel took their toll and Savage lay on top of the bed and within moments a soft snore filled the room.

★ ★ ★

Screaming dragged Savage from the depths of sleep. Ear-piercing shrieks came from one of the other rooms.

'Amy!' he cried out as he came

awake, then remembered where he was.

There was a man's voice as well as the woman's screams. An angry voice. Then Savage heard another voice. A woman's this time, more urgent and quite frantic.

As the fog in Savage's mind cleared he heard another man's voice. This one he recognized as West, the saloon owner. The gunshot that sounded next was followed by screams for help.

This time, his reaction was automatic and Savage came off the bed and took the Remington from the holster. He opened the door and stepped into the hall to see a whore on her knees beside an obviously dead West.

Lilly looked up at Savage and though the light in the hallway was dim, the glisten of tears on her cheeks was unmistakeable.

'Help us please Mister,' she begged. 'Otherwise, he'll kill Clementine. He's already gone and killed Ernie.'

Grim-faced, Savage thumbed back the hammer on the Remington and stepped into the open doorway. The man stood over a cowering woman in the corner with his hand raised to strike again.

'Do it and I'll kill you,' Savage warned him, his voice full of menace.

Ross froze and looked over his shoulder at the semi-naked man holding the gun on him.

'This don't concern you, stranger. The bitch was tryin' to rob me and I'm just givin' her what she deserves.'

'I say she's had enough. Leave her be.'

'How about you mind your own damned business before you start somethin' you can't finish,' Ross threatened. 'Now turn around and walk away.'

With total disdain for the presence of the cocked six-gun, Ross made to lash Clementine once more. His fist started to fall but never landed.

Savage squeezed the trigger. One shot was all it took and Ross lurched forward and fell in a heap on the floor, like a marionette with its strings cut.

He waited a few moments to see if the man moved and when he didn't, Savage stepped back out into the hall.

'Thank you, Mister,' Lilly sobbed as she climbed to her feet. 'Is he . . . ?'

'He won't be givin' you anymore trouble,' Savage assured her.

Without another word she hurried into the room to check on Clementine. She gasped loudly when she saw the state of her friend then rushed back out the door and spotted Esther. 'Get Doc Martin. Quick.'

Esther ran off and a short time later a commotion sounded from the stairs. Savage was about to step back inside his room when a large man with gray hair and a badge pinned to his chest appeared.

'What in tarnation is goin' on here?' Miller's irritation was etched all over his face. Then he saw West's body on the floor. 'Aww, hell no.'

He shifted his gaze to Savage. 'You, start talkin'.'

'A feller in that room there,' Savage pointed to the open door, 'was beatin' up on one of the girls. He shot West who tried to stop him.'

'And then what?' Miller snapped.

'He wouldn't stop so I shot him.'

'Just like that?'

'Yeah,' Savage nodded. 'Just like that.'

'What's your name?'

'Savage.'

'Wait here, Savage,' Miller ordered and walked past West's corpse and into the room where Lilly was tending to Clementine.

There was movement behind Savage and the doctor brushed past him followed by Esther. They were about to enter the room when Miller emerged and said in a low voice, 'Ain't no hurry Seth, she's dead.'

A low keening sound came from the room as Lilly broke down and Esther hurried in to comfort her while Martin bent and double-checked West.

Miller came back to Savage and said, 'Come by my office later. I may have a few more questions for you.'

'OK,' Savage agreed. 'I had plans on comin' to see you anyways.'

Miller cocked an eyebrow. 'Why's that?'

'I'm lookin' for a feller I was told is in town,' he explained. 'His name is Clint Ross.'

There was something in Miller's expression that changed and he inquired, 'Have you ever seen this Ross before?'

'Nope.'

Miller snorted. 'Well if that don't beat all. That feller in there just happens to be the one you're lookin' for. His name was Clint Ross.'

6

Savage felt his blood run cold at the mention of Ross' name. Sure, he'd got what was coming to him but Savage had questions that needed answers; and he'd wanted him to know the name of the man who was going to kill him, and why.

'What about the feller he came to town with?' Savage asked, trying to keep his emotions in check.

'Cody? I ain't seen him for a day or so, but he'll be around.'

Another name on the list.

'What did you want Ross for anyhow?' Miller inquired.

'I had a couple of questions for him,' Savage told the sheriff. 'Guess it don't much matter now.'

Miller shook his head. 'I knew these fellers were goin' to be trouble. My advice to you Savage, leave town as soon as you can. Or maybe you'll be havin' trouble with Ross' pard.'

Then Miller noticed his pants. 'Or them Yankee blues you're wearin' will buy you some.'

'War's over, Sheriff,' Savage said pointedly. 'Or ain't you noticed?'

'It may well be, Savage but folks around here have long memories.'

'Yeah, well, they'll just have to get over it, won't they?'

'Fair enough, but what about Cody?'

'Tell him where to find me,' Savage snapped. 'I'll be downstairs sittin' at a table waitin' for him.'

With that, he turned and stalked back into his room.

★　★　★

Savage got no more sleep that night. He sat on his bed and waited for morning as he mulled over his options. He thought about the war, about Carver, and about Amy.

When the orange fingers of the new

day reached out across the sky, Savage rose from his bed and dressed, his belly a knot of emotion at the anticipation of facing one of his wife's killers. The last thing to go on was the gunbelt with the Remington in the holster.

Once downstairs, Savage had his pick of the tables because all were vacant. He doubted somehow that the Golden Garter would even open today due to the untimely demise of its owner. So he took a pack of cards off the bar and sat down at a table in the center of the room facing the door.

Next, he took the Remington from its holster and lay it on the tabletop. Then he waited.

Savage wiled away the time playing solitaire. There were some noises from upstairs but two hours passed before a woman's voice said, 'You know the saloon ain't goin' to open today, don't you, Cowboy?'

Savage looked up and saw the woman who'd begged him for his help, standing on the stairs. 'I ain't here for a drink. I'm waitin' to see a man.'

Lilly descended the rest of the way and walked gracefully across to the bar. She wore a floor-length green dress that covered her ample chest. Her pale white arm reached over and grabbed a half-empty bottle of whiskey and two glasses.

She carried them to the table where Savage sat and placed them in the center. She pulled back a chair and joined him. Her delicate hands with brightly painted fingernails popped the cork on the bottle and poured out two drinks. She pushed one over in front of Savage.

Lilly picked hers up and said, 'Here's to Ernie.'

She tossed the liquid back and didn't bat an eyelid.

Savage picked his up and did the same.

'You want another, Cowboy?'

Savage shook his head. 'One will be fine. And it's Savage.'

'I'm Lilly,' she told him. 'By the way,

90

Savage, I didn't get the chance to thank you for tryin' to help Clementine.'

He studied her for a brief moment and came to the conclusion that she was quite pretty. However, if she spent much more time in her line of work, that would certainly change and it wouldn't matter how well her long black hair framed her face.

Savage remained silent.

'Who are you waitin' for?' Lilly inquired.

'Cody.'

Lilly was mortified. 'Ross' friend? Why?'

'I need to ask him some questions.'

'But he'll more than likely try to kill you for shootin' his friend,' she pointed out.

Their conversation was interrupted as someone hammered on the door loud enough to make Lilly start, then a voice called out, 'Open up damn it.'

'I guess we're about to find out,' Savage surmised.

Savage looked over at the whore, 'Let

him in and take a few steps back. Make sure you stay out of the way.'

Lilly got up and walked slowly to the door. She went to open it and hesitated.

'It's OK,' Savage assured her. 'Open it and step back.'

Lilly nodded and did as she was asked.

Cody barged in and stopped short when he saw Savage.

'Are you the son of a bitch who shot Ross?' he snarled.

With his right hand resting on the Remington, Savage said, 'I am.'

Cody's blue eyes blazed. 'Then it's time you met the same fate.'

'Hold it, Cody,' came Sheriff Miller's voice from the doorway.

Cody whirled. 'You stay the hell out of this lawman,' Cody warned and turned back to face Savage.

'Before you go for that gun of yours I want to ask you somethin',' Savage said. 'Have you been to Summerton lately?'

The outlaw's eyes widened and his hand slashed down for his six-gun.

Savage had the advantage as the Remington was already cocked and in his hand, and had only to pull the trigger.

The .44 slug hit Cody in his gun arm halfway between shoulder and elbow and smashed the bone. The outlaw dropped his gun at his feet and cried out with pain.

The hammer ratcheted back as Savage cocked the Remington again. He sighted on Cody's left leg and squeezed the trigger. Thunder rocked the room and a bright red blossom appeared on the outlaw's thigh.

Cody screamed with pain and collapsed to the floor. Savage stood up and slowly crossed to where the outlaw squirmed in pain.

Cody looked up at the figure who towered over him and said through gritted teeth, 'What now?'

'I want to know where Carver was goin'?' Savage asked.

'I don't know.'

The hammer on the Remington went

back with a loud triple-click.

'Just hold on a damned minute, Savage,' Miller protested. 'What do you think you're doin'?'

'Ever heard of John Carver, Miller?' Savage asked the sheriff.

'Sure,' he said, nodding.

'Well Ross and this hombre here are part, or were part of his gang,' Savage explained, his voice growing harsh. 'A while back, Carver hit a small town called Summerton and cleaned out the bank.'

'I heard somethin' along those lines,' Miller allowed.

'There was a bloody shootout in the main street and some good people died,' Savage continued. 'When they left town they took a young woman with them. She just happened to be my wife. I found her body myself. What they did to her before they damn well killed her was inhumane.'

Lilly's hand flew to her mouth in horror at the mental imagery. 'Oh, lord.'

'I found out Ross was comin' here and as luck would have it, albeit bad, I happened to shoot him last night before I found out who he was or could ask him some questions. But now I have Cody and he's able to talk.'

'This ain't the way, Savage,' Miller said.

'Wrong Miller. It's the only way. You can have him after I've finished.'

'Son . . . ?'

'They raped and murdered my wife,' Savage spat venomously. 'And right now I want to know where the rest of them are. So don't get in my way.'

Miller saw the look in Savage's eyes and knew the only way to stop him would be to shoot him. And he didn't want to do that, especially if what he said was true.

'Why isn't Matt Bryson trailin' 'em?' Miller asked.

'You know him?'

'Yeah.'

'He's dead. They killed him.'

Savage turned back to Cody. 'Where

was Carver goin'?'

Cody looked at him defiantly. 'You ain't goin' to shoot me. Not with the law standin' there watchin' you.'

The Remington roared and blood spouted from the outlaw's right knee. Cody screamed as he writhed on the floor.

'Answer me God damn it!' Savage roared.

Cody glanced at Miller, his eyes pleading for the lawman to intervene. 'Help me, please. He's crazy. I . . . '

The outlaw's voice trailed away when Miller turned away and started towards the stairs.

'Let me know when you're done,' he said to Savage. 'Come on, Lilly, you don't need to see this.'

That was all it took for the outlaw to breakdown. Within minutes Savage found out that the others had scattered.

Duane Brooks was headed for a mining town called Silver Ridge in the Big bend Country. Chase Hunter was going to Presidio where his father had a ranch. Carver, Thomas, and Cooper were aiming for New Mexico.

'What about Anderson White?' Savage asked Cody.

'He's dead,' Cody told him. 'He picked up a bullet when we hit the bank. The blood poisonin' killed him.'

Savage stared at Cody with cold, emotionless eyes. 'Did you take your turn?'

'What?'

'Did you take your turn with my wife?'

'Hell no,' Cody answered, eyes wide with panic. 'I didn't touch your wife.'

'But you didn't stop them either, did you?' Savage shot back.

The outlaw's mouth opened and closed but no sound came out.

'Pick up your gun,' Savage told him in a low voice.

'What? No.'

'Pick it up. It's the only chance you'll get,' Savage warned him. 'I'm goin' to shoot you whether you pick it up or not. The choice is yours.'

'But that's not fair,' Cody whined.

Savage bristled. 'And do you think it was fair that my wife was so brutally taken away from me? You have until I count three.'

'But . . . '

'One.'

' . . . You . . . '

'Two.'

Cody's panicked expression changed into that of a cornered animal. A snarling, snapping beast with nowhere to go. Then he lunged for his six-gun.

No sooner had Cody's fingers wrapped around the gun-butt, when Savage's Remington roared, its .44 caliber slug smashed into the outlaw's head and out the back, blood and bone sprayed across the floor.

Smoke drifted from the six-gun's barrel in thin tendrils. Savage holstered it and looked to the top of the stairs where Miller stood gazing down upon the killer and the corpse.

'You got a problem with that?'

Miller shook his head. 'Nope. He went for his gun. I saw it all.'

Savage looked down at Cody's body

and cursed inwardly. He thought he was done with killing after the war. Since the war had finished, he'd killed five men and knew that there was more to come.

'I need a drink,' he said hoarsely and walked towards the bar.

* * *

When Savage awoke the following morning, his head felt as though a hard-rock miner was on the inside trying to hammer his way out with a pick. He moaned involuntarily as he glanced at the bright sunshine that streamed in through a crack in the curtain. His mouth was dry, as though full of hot desert sands.

He should have damn well left the day before. However, the drinking had helped ease the pain, helped him to forget, albeit briefly. He swung his legs over the bed and sat up, disturbing the woman in the bed beside him.

Savage glanced back at the still

sleeping Lilly. The sheet had slipped down and exposed her top half. Her dark hair was mussed and straggled down over the milky white skin of her bare shoulders and large breasts. He reached over and pulled the sheet back up.

He cursed his weakness for sleeping with her, his momentary lapse in judgment, but the time spent in her arms had been another way to forget the horror of the past ten days or so.

He stood up and walked quietly over to his clothes draped over the chair, and dressed.

'Tryin' to sneak out on me, Cowboy?' asked Lilly's drowsy voice as he strapped on his gun belt.

He turned to face the bed and saw her propped up on an elbow looking at him.

'I . . . I . . . ' he stammered.

'It's alright,' she said trying to ease his mind. 'We both got what we needed from it.'

Savage felt embarrassed and dug into

his pants pocket for some money to give her.

'Don't you dare think about paying me,' she said indignantly.

He stuffed the money back into his pocket. 'Sorry.'

Savage looked at himself in the mirror as he put his hat on. Still unshaven, the growth had transformed into a dark beard. A changed look for a changed man.

He glanced one final time at Lilly and said, 'Maybe I'll see you around.'

'Maybe, Cowboy. Maybe.'

He shut the door gently as he left the room.

7

It was a harsh, baked part of Texas. A landscape of jagged, rocky peaks surrounded by great expanses of rugged desert with creosote, yucca, mesquite, and other hardy plants adapted to the conditions.

It was also a landscape of hidden dangers. Mexican bandits, outlaws, and Mescalero Apaches roamed freely, killing and looting.

Savage was two weeks out of Buckley and half a day from Silver Ridge when he came across an upturned stage.

It was on its side just off the trail. The first sign of something wrong was the circling buzzards high in the sky, gradually getting lower in lazy spirals.

Savage stopped the bay in the center of the trail and leaned down to take the Winchester from its scabbard. He levered a round into the breech automatically while alert eyes scanned the immediate area for any sign of trouble.

Beneath him, the horse shifted nervously, sensing the tension in its rider's body.

Earlier in the day, Savage had seen a smudge of dust to the west. A number of years before the war, even before he'd settled down, he'd worked with a freight company who'd shipped through this part of Texas. The outfit had tangled with Apaches on more than one occasion so he knew that dust rising from that direction could mean but one thing, trouble.

He pulled off the trail and into a deep dry wash. After he dismounted, he took the Winchester and crawled back up the embankment to wait in the baking sun. Even the lizards were hiding from it.

Almost thirty minutes later, a handful of Mescalero Apache appeared and started riding parallel with the trail. His caution had paid off.

He waited another half hour to make

sure they were gone and led the horse back up onto the trail. The problem now was that they were headed in the same direction.

When he came across the ghastly scene, the six-up stage team was all down but still in harness. The stage was tipped on its side and the driver and guard lay in the middle of the road. Both had been shot full of arrows and scalped.

Savage climbed down from the bay and walked over to the stage. Above the door was a hand-painted sign which read: *Silver Ridge Stage Lines.*

He looked inside and saw that the passengers were dead. Both were male and had been well armed.

Savage stepped back from the coach and examined the ground around him and it struck him that things seemed to be too clean. Someone had taken the time to erase all traces of disturbance.

Something seemed not right. If it were Mescaleros, why kill all of the horses? Why leave guns and ammunition on the men in the coach? And why . . . ? he stopped. There in the dust as clear as day, was a heeled boot print.

Off to his left, a quail took flight, flapping furiously as it launched itself from a clump of creosote.

Savage froze. Something had startled it and his immediate conclusion was the Mescaleros he'd seen earlier. His first thought was for his horse and then the Winchester. Although he had the Remington on his hip, it only carried six shots. Trying to reload while he had Apaches trying to lift his hair could prove fatal. The Winchester, on the other hand, had fifteen shots and would be ideal.

Only ten yards stood between him and the bay. He turned and walked slowly towards it. A flutter of movement to his right caught his eye.

Without hesitation, he dived and rolled. An arrow whistled past overhead and flew harmlessly into the surrounding desert.

Savage completed the roll by coming

up on one knee as another arrow stuck into the earth in front of him. The Remington came out in a fluid draw as he sought a target.

From the brush in front of him emerged an Apache, dressed in a loin cloth, shirt, and knee-high moccasins. He was armed with a bow and paused to draw the string back.

Savage snapped a shot off in his direction and the Indian cried out with pain. He dropped the bow and clutched at his stomach. Another .44 slug finished him off.

Turning, Savage lunged towards the mare in a desperate play to get the Winchester. A gunshot sounded and he felt the round pass close. *Damn it*, he cursed to himself. At least one of them had a gun of some description.

His hand slapped the stock of the Winchester and Savage ripped it from the saddle scabbard. He whirled and saw that two more Apaches had emerged from the desert landscape. One of them was the warrior with the gun, a rifle. These were closer this time and he could see their paint-daubed faces.

Hurriedly, Savage jacked a round into the Winchester's breech. He threw it to his shoulder and fired at the Apache with the gun but wasn't quick enough to stop him firing.

The slug from the Mescalero's rifle missed, though not by much. There was a hollow *thunk* behind him and the mare let out a high-pitched shriek of pain. The slug Savage fired, however, didn't miss and the Apache was flung back by the .44 caliber slug. He flopped like a rag doll into the dry desert sand and didn't move.

Shifting his aim, Savage worked the lever and fired once more. Again he was too late and the arrow loosed by the Mescalero scored a bloody furrow along his left rib cage. It made him flinch and the shot that he fired flew wide.

Working the lever again, Savage lined the foresight upon the Indian's chest and squeezed the trigger. The kick from the Winchester drove back against his shoulder and through the gun smoke that partly obscured his vision, he saw the Apache fall.

Three down, and by Savage's calculations, there should be two more. With the Winchester still tucked against his shoulder he looked for the others but saw no one. Then he heard the drum of hoofbeats that faded in the distance. They had left.

Savage remembered the bay and spun about to see the mare on the ground. He hurried to her and knelt by her side and examined her wound. Her breathing was labored and she had a rattle deep within. The stray bullet had entered just behind her fore-shoulder on the right side. There was nothing more to be done so he got to his feet and placed the muzzle of the Winchester an inch from her forehead and squeezed the trigger. As the adrenaline started to wear off, Savage suddenly became aware of the burning sensation on his left side. He looked down and saw the bloody tear in his shirt.

Now he was afoot in the desert. Unless . . .

He walked over to the brush where the Apaches had come from, checking their bodies as he went just to make sure.

Savage walked through the mesquite about twenty yards then it opened out into a small clearing. There, hobbled together, were three horses. In their rush to get away, the remaining Mescaleros had left them behind.

Two were wiry Indian ponies and the other was a sorrel. He chose the latter because it was most likely the one to be saddle-broke then set the others free.

After a brief struggle, Savage managed to retrieve his saddle from the bay and onto the sorrel along with the rest of his gear. Once he was finished, he climbed up onto the horse. At first, it skittered sideways at the unfamiliar rider but once he was aboard, the animal was fine.

He turned the horse towards Silver Ridge and put it into a loping canter. With any luck, he'd reach town before the sun dropped below the horizon.

★ ★ ★

The main street of Silver Ridge showed two typical architectural styles. The timber structures had large false-fronts that hid buildings of varying sizes.

In contrast to these were the adobe buildings built with a mixture of mud and straw or even manure made into bricks, then were slow dried in the shade to reduce cracking.

Three of the timber buildings were saloons. Each establishment had its name on a large hand-painted sign above their second-floor windows. The Cactus Rose, the Mine King, and the Lucky Strike.

People stopped on boardwalks to stare curiously at the stranger dressed in the cavalry pants and buckskin jacket, then went on about their business doing last minute jobs before the sun went down.

Silver Ridge stood at the foot of the Chisos Mountains and had come about from a silver strike six years before. It was surrounded by miles and miles of desert country and the town's main water source was a spring that rose near the edge of town.

The first stop on Savage's agenda was to the local sheriff. He needed to inform the law about the stage he'd found earlier in the afternoon and while he was there, he would ask about Brooks. After that, he would see to the sorrel.

The last red rays of sunlight were stretched out across the sky when Savage found what he was searching for.

The Silver Ridge law office was a plain timber building with a veranda out front. It was double story with the jail cells upstairs. It also had a large sign painted in bold red letters that said, *Sheriff's Office.*

Savage looped the reins over the hitching rail out front and wearily climbed the steps. He crossed the boardwalk and walked in through the door.

'Can I help you, stranger?' a tall man with red hair asked.

Savage nodded. 'You can if you're the sheriff.'

'Tip Morton,' he greeted. 'And you are . . . ?'

'Jeff Savage,' Savage offered as he looked around the jail. It was a sparsely furnished space with two chairs, a scarred desk, a gun rack on the wall and a cabinet for papers. In the corner was a pot-bellied stove and the room was lit by a single lamp.

But it was the stove that interested Savage the most. Or the smell of freshly brewed coffee that emanated from the battered pot on top.

'What can I do for you, Savage?'

'I could use a coffee if you don't mind.'

Morton stared blankly at him for a

moment then nodded.

'Alright,' Morton said and he found a cup and tossed it to Savage. 'Help yourself and while you're at it start talkin'.'

As he poured the steaming liquid into the cup, Savage said, 'About half a day out I came across an upturned coach. Sign on it said it was a Silver Ridge stage.'

'Damn it,' Morton cursed. 'The bastards have done it again. It was Apaches wasn't it?'

'It looked that way,' Savage allowed. 'But . . . '

'Hang on a moment,' Morton said stopping him. Then he called out, 'Shelby? Get in here.'

A young man entered from a back room. He was medium size and build and had a badge pinned to his vest.

'What's up, Tip?'

'Go and get Baxter and Wheeler,' Morton ordered. 'They'll be at the Cactus Rose. Tell 'em that it is to do with the stage.'

'Again?' asked Shelby raising his eyebrows in surprise.

'Yes, again. Now get goin'.'

The young deputy rushed out the door and was gone.

Morton turned his attention back to Savage and explained, 'Morg Baxter owns the stage lines and Hap Wheeler bosses the Silver Bullet mine. If you're goin' to tell me what you found then you may as well tell them at the same time. Saves you repeatin' yourself.'

'Fair enough,' Savage agreed. 'While we're waitin' for 'em maybe you can tell me somethin'?'

'If I can.'

'Duane Brooks, do you know him?'

'Yeah,' Morton allowed. 'I know him. Wild one like his brother. Haven't seen him since he rode out to fight in the war, though. Why?'

'I heard tell he was comin' back here and I thought I might look him up,' Savage lied and took a sip of his coffee.

Morton looked at Savage suspiciously.

'What about his brother, might he know?'

'If you can find him,' Morton snorted. 'Though if he shows his face around here I'll lock him up.'

'Why?'

Morton was about to explain more when Shelby returned with Baxter and Wheeler.

'Damn it to hell, Tip,' the middle-aged Wheeler fumed. 'Shelby says it's happened again. Is it true?'

'It appears so,' Morton confirmed. 'Savage here found the stage.'

'Well man, out with it,' the solidly built Baxter snapped. 'Tell us what you found.'

'Before you start, there is one thing you should know, Savage,' Morton interrupted. 'There was ten thousand in silver on that coach.'

That would explain their behavior, Savage thought to himself.

Savage told the men about the events of the day including the gunfight with the Mescaleros.

'Good show,' Wheeler sneered. 'That'll teach the bastards to steal the company silver. Was there any sign of it?'

Savage shook his head. 'Nope. And I don't think it was Mescaleros who stole the silver and killed those men either.'

As Savage drank the last of his coffee all eyes turned in his direction questioningly.

'But you just told us that the men were scalped, shot full of arrows, and to top it off they damn well attacked you where it happened.' Baxter reminded him furiously.

'That's right,' Savage acknowledged.

'Well, hell,' Wheeler snapped. 'I don't know about you Savage, but from where I'm standin', that is a mighty strong case. Don't know how you drew your conclusion.'

'You'd better explain yourself, Savage,' Morton urged him. 'What makes you so sure it weren't Mescaleros?'

'First off, tell me about the other robbery.'

'It was pretty much the same as the

116

one you've just told us about,' Morton elaborated. 'Horses shot, men scalped and shot full of arrows.'

'Anything else to suggest Apaches done it? Any tracks?'

'What more do you want?' Baxter snorted derisively.

Savage ignored him and Morton said, 'There were no tracks at all. But that's somethin' the Apaches would do, blot out their tracks. They wouldn't want us followin' them back to their camp.'

'That's true,' Savage agreed. 'But before the war, I worked with a freight outfit that used to run through the Big Bend country and we tangled with the Apaches some. And . . . '

'And what?' Wheeler interrupted sarcastically. 'Get to the point.'

'And there are four things I learned about them.'

'Like what?' Wheeler snapped impatiently.

'One is that Apache just don't shoot horses for somethin' to do. They just take 'em. Yeah, they might shoot one to stop the coach but not all of them,' Savage pointed out. 'Two is, why didn't they take the guns and ammunition? The ones that attacked me had one rifle between them. If it was them then they sure as hell needed them. The third is why would they take the silver? They don't need it.'

'And the fourth?' Baxter asked.

'Is when did Mescaleros start wearin' heeled boots?'

8

A heavy silence descended over the room as the four men took in what Savage had just told them. He waited while they were deep in thought.

It was Morton who broke the silence.

'Could it have been someone from the stage?'

'All of the tracks were wiped out, even around the bodies,' Savage explained. 'Except they missed one. A heeled boot with a square toe and a piece out of the sole.'

'And you're sure that it wasn't the Mescaleros that done it?' Wheeler asked.

'As sure as I can be without being witness to the robbery itself,' Savage assured him.

'That does it,' Wheeler snapped furiously. 'It has to be him. That son of a bitch came back like he said he would.'

'Hold hard there, Hap,' Morton

advised the mine boss. 'You can't be sure.'

'It has to be who?' Savage inquired.

'Elmo Brooks,' Wheeler seethed. 'The bastard said he'd be back after I fired him from the mine. He was skimmin' some of the silver. But of course, we couldn't prove it so I fired him anyway.'

'He's always been trouble,' Baxter nodded.

Savage's ears pricked. 'What about his brother, Duane.'

'I already told you, he ain't been around here since before the war,' Morton reiterated.

'What are we goin' to do, Hap?' Baxter asked. 'There's another shipment you want gone in a few days. This one's even bigger. Twenty thousand. Maybe we should postpone it.'

Savage thought quickly. He was certain that if this was the work of Elmo Brooks, then his brother wouldn't be far away.

'No.'

All eyes turned to Savage.

'What do you mean no?' Morton asked.

'What would you say if I said I could get the ones responsible for it all?' Savage asked.

'How do you propose to do that all on your lonesome?' Wheeler asked sceptically.

'I didn't say I could do it all on my own,' Savage pointed out. 'You fellers will have to do your bit.'

'I ain't so sure,' Baxter's voice filled with uncertainty. 'Why should we trust you?'

Savage shrugged. 'No reason at all.'

'Alright, I'm listening,' said Wheeler.

'I am too,' muttered Morton. 'This should be interesting.'

'I want you to find five men that'll follow orders and make sure they are trustworthy,' Savage told them. 'Oh, and they need to be able to shoot.'

'Why can't you find 'em?' Wheeler asked.

'Look at me, Wheeler. I'm dressed mostly in Union blue and we're in

Texas. You work it out.'

'Alright, what else?'

'Just do everythin' like normal,' Savage explained. 'We'll leave the night before the shipment and wait a few miles outside of town. After the stage has gone past we'll shadow it.'

'Why do you think they'll hit the next one?' Shelby asked.

Savage settled his steely gaze on him. 'Because someone is givin' 'em information from the inside, that's why.'

'I find that hard to believe,' Wheeler snorted.

'Well, how do you expect they found out about the shipments if they ain't in town?' Savage asked him. 'They sure as shootin' ain't mind readers.'

'I don't like it,' Baxter stated. 'All your plan does is put more of my men in danger.'

'It's a chance you'll have to take.'

'No, it ain't.'

'Aww hell, Baxter,' Wheeler snapped. 'I'll supply the damned men for the job.'

'What do you get out of this deal?' Morton asked.

'$1,000 dollars and a chance to kill a man who needs killin',' Savage said matter of factly.

The penny dropped for Morton. 'Duane Brooks?'

'Yeah.'

'But you don't even know if he's with 'em,' Morton pointed out. 'We don't even know if Elmo is behind it. What makes you want him so bad for anyways?'

Savage's voice grew cold. 'The son of a bitch was part of a bunch of killers who were responsible for the murder of my wife. Their boss was John Carver.'

'Don't make this some sort of damn revenge ride, Savage,' Morton warned.

'Too late,' he told the sheriff and turned to Wheeler and Baxter. 'So, do you want my help or not?'

There was a brief silence as both men looked at each other then nodded. 'Yes.'

'Fine then. When is the shipment going?'

'Four days,' Wheeler answered.

Savage nodded. 'Can you get the men together by tomorrow night?'

'Should be no problem.'

'Just remember to keep it quiet,' Savage cautioned them. 'Or it may be us that end up on the wrong side of the ambush.'

★ ★ ★

At around nine the following evening there was a knock on the door of Savage's small hotel room. Seven men filed in and took up positions about the room.

'You didn't tell us we'd be takin' up with a damn Yank,' one of the men said bitterly.

'Hold your tongue, Levi,' Wheeler snapped.

'He's got a point,' another man pointed out.

'Shut it all of you,' Wheeler ordered. 'Once I've told you what is goin' on then you can make up your own minds.'

124

The room grew quiet after a few more murmurings.

'Right, now let's get started,' Wheeler stated. 'As you know another load of silver was taken. This time, off the stage we shipped it on.'

'Blasted Indians,' the man called Levi muttered.

'It wasn't Indians.'

The five newcomers looked at Savage.

'Says who?' Levi demanded.

'I do,' Savage said firmly. 'Now shut up and listen or get your ass out the door. We're here to work together, not fight the damn war all over again. However, if you still feel as though you need to, come and see me after the job is done and I'll accommodate you.'

Levi glared at him for a time before he smiled mirthlessly. 'Alright, I can wait.'

'Now the pleasantries are out of the way I'll introduce everyone,' Wheeler said, a hint of sarcasm in his voice. 'Levi you know, the others are Curtis, Wallace, Edmonds, and lastly Roy Horton.'

As each man's name was said, Savage

eyed them all carefully.

Wheeler continued. 'This gentleman is Savage. And before you ask, yes he is in charge and you will take orders from him.'

They didn't like it but remained silent.

Savage explained what he wanted from them and his exploits when he found the stage. By the time he was finished their expressions had softened a little.

'How much are you men gettin' paid for this?' he asked them.

'A hundred dollars a man,' Curtis answered.

Shifting his gaze to Wheeler, Savage said flatly, 'Each man gets a thousand dollars.'

'The hell you say,' Wheeler spluttered.

'They get it or I don't help you out,' Savage said bluntly. 'Their lives are worth as much as mine.'

Wheeler wanted to protest more but instead nodded. 'OK.'

The five men kept their faces passive but Savage could see the surprise in their eyes.

'How many of you served?'

'All of us,' said the short Edmonds.

'Who's the best shot amongst you all?'

'Levi,' Curtis answered. 'He was a sharpshooter.'

It would be, thought Savage.

'Be ready to ride tomorrow night,' he told them. 'And say nothing. Better still, if you can get out of town individually and meet up outside of town, even better.'

Savage paused before he asked, 'Any questions?'

No one spoke.

'Alright then, I'll see you tomorrow night.'

As they started to file out of the room, Savage said, 'Levi, you stay.'

The man glared coldly at him but did as he was bid. Once everyone was gone and the door closed he scowled.

'What do you want with me, Yank?'

he asked bitterly.

'Drop the attitude,' Savage snapped and immediately thought of his time in the cavalry. 'Were you any good as a sharpshooter?'

'Good enough.'

'Well then, I have a job for you. It'll be dangerous and it could get you killed. Think you might be up to it?'

'Depends on what it is.'

'What gun did you use in the war? A Whitworth?'

Levi frowned. 'Yeah.'

'You still got it?'

'Uh huh.'

'Here's what I want you to do,' Savage explained. 'I want you gone from here before dawn in the morning. I'm taking a gamble that when they hit the next shipment it'll be in the same place as the last. What I want you to do is take that rifle of yours and find a place there to hole up.'

'Why?'

'Because, although we'll be shadow-ing the shipment, we won't be close enough to stop them if they start killin' those on board,' Savage explained. 'If it looks like that is about to happen, then you can start shootin' from long range.'

Levi nodded his understanding.

'Be aware of the Apaches as well,' Savage warned, 'You'll be on your own so be careful and stay out of sight.'

'I'll be fine,' Levi told him.

*   *   *

The former sharpshooter left before dawn the following morning. Savage was confident that he would be fine. He'd be used to being out on his own in dangerous situations.

The rest left the following night as planned. They met outside of town and after a few questions regarding the missing Levi they rode off.

The stage which had been retrieved along with the bodies of the dead was repaired and left the next morning. The driver, shotgun messenger, and two guards had not been briefed on the plan. The fewer that knew the better the chances of taking the stage robbers by surprise.

9

The tell-tale smudge of dust on the horizon told Levi that the stage was on approach. Yet he wasn't the only one to see it. There were six riders below his position who had also caught sight of the dust cloud.

Levi had arrived there around noon the day before and found a place to hole up around 500 yards off the trail. He was situated on a low ridge amongst some large jagged rock outcrops and creosote bush. It was enclosed enough for good cover but open enough for a clear field of fire.

He'd tied his horse at the foot of the backside of the ridge then made himself comfortable for the wait.

Levi thought about his horse laying dead where he'd been hobbled. Earlier that morning, soon after sunrise a band of twenty Mescalero's had ridden close by on the backside of the ridge.

As soon as his horse caught the scent of the other horses he'd started to get fractious. Rather than have the Indians become aware that he was about, Levi had chosen to do something he felt was his only option. He quickly scrambled off the ridge, placed a hand over the animal's muzzle, and with his knife, had slashed its throat.

He hated doing it but knew it was better than being slow-roasted.

The Apaches rode on blissfully unaware of the white man upon the ridge.

The six outlaws arrived just after noon and took up their positions in the brush to the side of the stage trail. Then they settled down to wait, with no knowledge or hint of the man who overlooked their position.

Levi's only problem after that were the vultures. The large carrion eaters who could smell out a meal from just about anywhere. It seemed that it was only a short while before the first one appeared, then another, and another. Circling high above and spiraling lower ever so gradually.

But before any attention could be drawn to the ridge and beyond, the smudge of dust had appeared.

Levi watched as it grew bigger until he could finally make out the stage at the base of the billowing cloud. It stood out like a giant beacon against the blue sky.

If the Mescaleros are still around they'll see that for sure, he thought to himself.

Down below, the outlaws readied themselves and as the stage drew closer they emerged from the brush and spread out across the trail to block the swaying vehicle's passage.

Levi could see the driver haul back on the reins and the stage was almost stopped when a gunshot sounded and the offside leader buckled.

The stage came to a lurching halt. The driver and shotgun messenger threw their hands into the air and both guards from the inside of the coach climbed out.

They threw their guns down and stood beside the stage. One of the outlaws ordered the other two down and soon all four men were grouped together on the rutted trail.

Levi slid the Whitworth rifle forward, cocked the hammer, and brought the rifle up to his shoulder. Its barrel rested on a metal fork to keep it steady.

The Whitworth rifle was actually a rifled musket of British manufacture. It had been used by Confederate sharpshooters in the civil war and fired a hexagonal .451 caliber bullet.

It had a range of 1,500 yards but was quite accurate anywhere up to 1,000. At 500 yards, Levi would have no trouble hitting whatever he aimed at, especially with its Davidson scope mounted on the side.

He watched in horror as one of the outlaws, still seated on his horse, raised a six-gun and fired at the driver. The flat report came quickly and the man was thrust backward and fell in a heap on the ground.

Levi trained the Whitworth on the shooter of the defenseless driver.

'Go to hell,' he whispered hoarsely and squeezed the trigger.

Elmo Brooks shifted his aim and lined the six-gun up on the messenger. He thumbed back the hammer and . . .

His head exploded.

By the time the bullet from the Whitworth punched into the outlaw's skull, the report finally reached the men's ears. Blood sprayed over an outlaw named Hudson who was beside Brooks' horse when his leader's head blew apart.

The six-gun fell from lifeless fingers and he toppled from the saddle and landed with a dull thud.

'Elmo!' Duane screeched at the sight of his brother's body.

'Where the hell did that come from?' one of the other outlaws shouted.

Duane Brooks whirled about and saw the pall of powder smoke that floated up from the ridge.

'Up there!' he shouted and pointed to where Levi was situated.

The former Confederate sharpshooter was a very competent man with the Whitworth, and due to limited numbers, only the best had been issued with one.

Though it was a musket and slow to reload, an experienced man like Levi could fire three rounds per minute. After twenty seconds, the rifle roared again.

This time, Hudson's chest blossomed red as the slug passed through and killed him instantly.

'Take cover!' Duane Brooks bellowed.

The four remaining outlaws dove for cover amid the rocks and brush just off the trail. The three men from the stage, surprised by the events, recovered and scooped up their own weapons. They took cover on the other side of the trail and started to fire at the outlaws.

Now they were trapped between two points of fire. As the battle began to heat up, neither side saw the rising dust cloud in the distance.

'I told you I heard gunfire!' Wallace exclaimed as the sound reached them.

'I guess you were right,' Savage declared and heeled the sorrel solidly.

It leaped forward from a trot into a gallop. The other men followed suit and soon left a large plume of dust in their wake.

The shots were louder now and they knew they had arrived. As they rounded the corner of the trail, the stage was there in front of them. Beside it lay the bodies of three men and Savage was instantly alarmed that they had arrived too late to save the men from the coach.

Without hesitation, Savage drew the Remington from its holster and led the men into the thick of battle.

From behind a rock, a man leaped to his feet and started to fire at the new arrivals. He managed two shots before Savage put him down with a slug to his torso.

Another man who was sheltered

behind a jagged rock raised up to fire, and a bullet from Wallace spun him around.

The outlaw went down on one knee, his body numb from the impact of the lead. The second shot from Wallace killed him.

There was a cry of pain to Savage's left. He glanced over in time to see Roy Horton crash to the ground with a slug in his chest.

Incensed at the sight of his friend going down, Curtis spurred his mount forward into the brush after the outlaw who'd fired the shot.

Savage saw him disappear, then his riderless horse emerged a short time later.

Cursing, Savage looked around for another target and found one, totally unaware that the man he was looking at was Duane Brooks.

While Savage was shooting at Brooks, Wallace whittled the outlaws down by one more, which left only two. Brooks and a tall outlaw called Black.

Suddenly, Savage's hammer fell on a spent chamber. Brooks looked at him and smiled coldly. He raised his gun and sighted on the helpless man in front.

The smile died on his face as a bullet from the Whitworth burst from his chest in a shower of red. Brooks lurched forward a few steps then halted. His mouth opened and blood flowed freely down his chin.

Like a tree being felled in a forest, he tilted forward and only stopped once his face hit the dirt.

'Don't shoot! the remaining outlaw screamed as he threw his hands up in surrender. 'I give up.'

The gunfire fell silent and Savage dismounted, his empty Remington still in his hand.

'What's your name?' he snapped.

'Black,' the outlaw answered. 'Clint Black.

'Who was your boss?'

'Elmo Brooks,' he told Savage.

'Where is he?'

Black pointed at the body on the trail.

'What about his brother?' Savage asked hopefully. 'Was he with you?' Without a word, Black indicated to the dead outlaw who'd almost killed Savage.

He went across and stared down at the open, sightless eyes of Duane Brooks. He stayed that way until the image was burned into his brain then he turned and walked away.

As he did so, Levi appeared from the brush carrying the Whitworth. Savage caught his eye and nodded. The ex-sharpshooter did the same. Neither spoke a word.

Savage kept walking.

Now there were four men left to kill.

★   ★   ★

Wheeler and Baxter couldn't have been happier with the outcome. So much so that they seemed to forget that three men had died bringing the outlaws to heel.

'Here's your money,' Wheeler said as

140

he tossed it on the worn desk in front of Savage. After his late return to town the night before, he'd slept fitfully then risen early and joined Wheeler and Baxter in Baxter's office at the stage depot. It was a small room, sparsely furnished, but with large windows which admitted ample light.

The money landed next to a quiver of arrows and a hand-crafted bow that he'd retrieved from one of the outlaw's horses.

Savage scooped up the bundle of notes and stuffed them in his pocket.

'Did them dead fellers have any family?'

'Why?' Wheeler asked cautiously.

'If they do, then they should get the money that's comin' to 'em,' Savage stated.

The mine manager was about to protest but thought better of it when he saw the expression on Savage's face.

'I'll see that they get it if there are any,' Wheeler said almost morosely.

'Did you fellers find out who was

givin' out the information?'

'We have a fair idea who it was,' Wheeler answered. 'That outlaw you brought in didn't know the man's name but he gave us a good description.'

'Where are you goin' from here?' Baxter asked.

'Over Presidio way,' Savage told him. 'There's another of Carver's men over there. His father has a ranch. Feller by the name of Hunter.'

Both men glanced at each other and Savage caught the look that passed between them.

'What is it?'

'This ranch, it wouldn't be the Bar-H now would it?' Baxter inquired.

Savage nodded. 'That's the name I was given.'

'You'd do well to stay away from there,' Wheeler warned him. 'Byron Hunter is a tough old coot with plenty of men to back his play. If it's his son you're after, maybe you should ride wary and take the long way around. Maybe . . . '

Wheeler's voice trailed away when he saw the expression on Savage's unshaven face.

'Maybe what?'

'All I'm sayin' is just be careful,' Wheeler told him by way of explanation. 'From what you told us, Hunter's son needs killin'. But to do that, you have to be alive. And he ain't all he seems to be.'

Savage was intrigued. 'How so?'

'Hunter has himself a big ranch over there, with lots of beef wanderin' the country.' Wheeler elaborated. 'Thing is, while the war was goin' on and not long after it, there was not much money in Texas beef. Still ain't. But Byron Hunter always seemed to have money. Word is that he was sellin' guns over the border.'

'That don't concern me.'

'Well it should,' Wheeler snapped. 'He's a bad man and if he gets so much as a sniff of what you're up to, then he'll take you apart.'

'Let him try.'

It wasn't a boast of bravado but an indication of how Savage felt. He was determined not to let anything get in the way of exacting his revenge on every one of his wife's killers.

Wheeler stepped forward and thrust out his right hand. 'Best of luck.'

'Thanks,' Savage said, taking the rough dry hand in his.

'Hope you get to finish what you started, Savage,' Baxter said genuinely. 'But like Wheeler says, watch yourself.'

'I plan to.'

Savage walked out of the office and saw Levi standing next to the hitching rail, waiting.

'Did you get your money?'

'Yeah,' Levi nodded. 'Are you leavin'?'

'Just as soon as I can.'

'You want some help?' the ex-sharpshooter asked.

At first, Savage was surprised and then he shook his head. 'Thanks, no. It's somethin' I gotta do on my own.'

Levi nodded that he understood. 'Yeah. Be careful.'

'I'll be seein' you,' Savage said.

'Yeah, maybe. Just do one thing. Get rid of them blue-belly duds you're wearin'. The next man who sees you wearin' 'em might not be as understandin' as me.'

Savage smiled. 'I'll think about it.'

Levi shrugged. 'It's your hide.'

The two men shook and Levi left him standing there. Savage was back on the trail before noon.

10

'Rider comin' in,' called a gangly cowboy who sat on the top rail of the corral.

Ten sets of eyes turned to look out across the flat at the stranger on the sorrel as he came closer to the ranch yard.

'Who is it?' called the solid, gray-haired man standing on the veranda of the large ranch house.

'Don't know Mr. Hunter,' shouted another cowboy. 'I ain't never seen him . . . Holy Hannah.'

'What is it?' Byron Hunter demanded.

'It's a damned Yank.'

'Get your rifles, boys,' Hunter ordered. 'We'll give the sonuver a warm Texas welcome.'

Each of the cowhands scrambled to-wards the bunkhouse to grab their rifles except for the one still on a bucking chestnut in the corral, breaking it.

'What's goin' on Pa?'

Byron turned and looked at his son. Chase was a tall man of twenty-five. He was thinly-built and had blond hair like his mother had had. But she was gone now. She took sick with a fever while her son was away at war and died.

'Got a rider comin' in,' Byron explained. 'A damned Yank.'

'What are you goin' to do?'

'Give him what for and send him packin',' the older Hunter explained. 'The boys are gettin' their guns.'

'This should be interestin',' Chase said, as his face split with a cold smile.

*　*　*

When Savage saw the cowboys make towards the bunkhouse, he knew there was going to be trouble. He dropped his hand to the Remington and left it resting there.

It had been five days since he'd left Silver Ridge. He'd stopped off at Presidio and been told where to find the Bar-H. He'd also learned that they were preparing for a trail drive.

Word had it that in June, about a month away, Charles Goodnight and Oliver Loving, were going to make a drive north. And Byron Hunter figured he'd follow along behind and cash in on the market that they opened up.

Except he wasn't going to take 2,000 head like they were. He had 4,000 head of longhorns he wanted moving. It may be the way in that Savage needed. He hoped.

Hunter would be hiring more hands for the drive and if he could get hired on, then he should be able to get his hands on Chase.

The first step was to get past the introductions.

From a distance, Savage could see that the ranch house was a solid, well-built, single-story building with a long veranda, on the end of which two men now stood.

His pulse quickened and he assumed that one of them would be the man he had come to kill.

Off to the right lay a long bunkhouse and the corral. The left side of the ranch yard held a large barn.

When the sorrel finally reached the hard-packed earth of the ranch yard, Savage was met by a wall of rifles, all pointed at him.

'You boys might want to point them guns somewhere else,' Savage remarked casually. 'I don't fancy gettin' fired before I'm hired.'

They all looked at him dumbly.

'What was that?' asked Byron Hunter as he moved forward off the veranda, his son by his side.

'I was told you were hirin' for a drive,' Savage told him. 'I'm lookin' for work.'

Chase Hunter snorted derisively. 'You sure got some nerve Yank. Ridin' in here like that. The last time I saw a feller looked like you, I filled him full of holes.'

There were a few sniggers from the cowhands.

Being brave in front of the hands,

Savage surmised.

'Was he runnin' away?' he retorted.

'Why you . . . ,' Chase snarled and clawed at the gun on his hip.

'You pull that thing and I'll kill you,' Savage's voice cracked.

Chase's hand froze, gun half drawn.

Savage was right, he had no spine.

'Like my son said, stranger, you sure got a nerve.'

Savage looked Byron Hunter in the eye. 'I only came here lookin' for a job Mr. Hunter. I don't want any trouble. If it's these clothes that bother you, the next time I shoot a feller wearin' 'em I won't keep 'em for myself. Only I didn't have a choice at the time.'

The elder Hunter stared him directly in the eye and Savage held his gaze. There was a pregnant pause and tension built before Hunter said, 'Do you know cows?'

'Pa . . . ' Chase blurted out but was cut off.

'Shut up Chase,' he snapped. 'If I want to hire this feller I will. Until you run this ranch, you'll take orders like the rest.'

It was then that Savage saw the look in Chase's eye. He may be a coward, but he was a dangerous coward. And he guessed that if he ever got up the courage, he'd shoot his father in the back.

'Well, Do you know cows?' Hunter asked again.

'Yeah I know cows.'

'What's your name?'

'Savage.'

'Savage what?'

'Just Savage.'

'Then you're hired,' Hunter said with finality. 'The men will show you the ropes. You'll get thirty a month and found. Payday is Saturday.'

'Obliged.'

★ ★ ★

'Where you from, Savage?' asked Morg Stanley, the ranch foreman that evening in the bunkhouse.

It was dim inside as the only illumination came from two lanterns which were all but useless.

'Rich Water,' Savage answered. 'Do you know it?'

'Know of it,' Stanley allowed. 'What brings you out this way?'

'Nothing left for me there,' Savage told him. 'So I just started driftin'. Heard tell that you fellers were makin' a drive and I needed money.'

'If you keep your nose clean you'll be fine,' Stanley told him. 'Just stay clear of Chase for a while.'

'What's put a burr under his saddle anyways?'

'Came back like that after the war,' the foreman explained. 'Mostly he's all yap but I wouldn't trust him. Neither should you.'

'Fine, I'll tread soft for a while,' Savage said, telling Stanley what he wanted to hear. 'But if he comes straight at me I ain't goin' to turn tail.'

Stanley caught the edge in his voice. 'I wouldn't expect you to. Turn in, we got an early start tomorrow.'

Later, as Savage lay in the dark on a lumpy mattress, he thought about Amy. About their wedding day and as always, the memories turned dark as he thought about her dying.

He'd make them all pay he thought bitterly. All of them.

Savage's first opportunity at Chase Hunter came two days later.

'You, Savage, get my horse and put a saddle on it,' Chase ordered. 'And hurry it up. I have work to do.'

It wasn't long after sunup and Savage and Stanley were getting ready to head out. Their job for the day was to look for strays in a part of the ranch the hands had already worked.

Savage just stared at Hunter without saying a word.

'Are you deaf or somethin'?'

He could sense the other hands watching him, their hands resting on six-guns, waiting to see what he would do.

In that moment, Savage wanted to

pull the Remington and kill Chase. Just do it and get it over with. But he was certain that the hands would shoot him down when it was done. Best he wait.

He turned away to tend to the sorrel.

'Don't you damn well turn your back on me,' Chase snarled and grasped Savage's left shoulder to spin him around.

Instead of resisting, Savage let himself be turned and once he was square on, his right fist streaked out like a striking rattler and sank into Chase's middle. All of his rage was channeled into the blow.

There was a loud whoosh of air as it exploded from Chase's lungs. The young man went weak at the knees, sank down and doubled over, trying to suck in much-needed air.

Savage knocked off Chase's hat and grabbed a fistful of blond hair. He dragged his antagonist's head up and cocked his fist ready to smash him in the face again.

'Savage,' Stanley snapped.

He turned his head to look at the ranch foreman, a wild look in his eyes. Then he saw the cocked six-gun in Stanley's hand.

'Let him go.'

Savage's hand opened and Chase fell back down on hands and knees.

'Just so you know,' Savage said through gritted teeth. 'If he does that again, I'll kill him.'

'Looks as though Chase ain't the only one with a burr under his saddle,' Stanley surmised. 'Get on your horse and ride. I'll catch you up.'

As the thunder of hooves faded, Chase managed to climb to his feet. His face screwed up into a look of hatred when he snarled, 'That son of a bitch is dead.'

'You might want to tread softly around him, Chase,' Stanley warned. 'I have me a feelin' he could chew you up and spit you out.'

'He won't even see it comin',' Chase murmured.

★ ★ ★

'Mind tellin' me what all that was about?' Stanley asked when he caught up with Savage.

'Weren't nothin',' Savage answered. 'He just learned that not everyone is goin' to take his bluster.'

'Nope,' said Stanley with a shake of his head. 'There was more to it than that. If I hadn't stopped you when I did, I reckon you'd have near killed him.'

'Maybe he deserved it,' Savage mumbled.

'What?'

'I said let's go and find these strays.'

Stanley watched Savage urge his mount to go faster. He had a nagging feeling that he hadn't heard the last of it and the conclusion would be the death of one or both men.

11

'Hold it right there, Gringo,' said a voice from behind Stanley. 'Keep your hands away from your guns or I will kill you.'

Stanley froze in front of the brush built gate he had been about to open to free a number of cattle penned up inside.

He was on foot and his horse was out of reach. He and Savage had split up to check separate brush-filled draws when he'd happened upon the makeshift yard with fifteen head in it.

Undoubtedly someone had worked hard to get them together and now he knew who.

Stanley turned slowly and stared at the smiling, unshaven face, split wide with a mirthless grin that showed yellowed teeth.

'Sanchez.' The name hissed from the

foreman's mouth.

'Si, it is me,' he then motioned about himself. 'And a few others.'

When Stanley looked he saw another four men emerge from the thick brush. A cold shiver ran down his spine. He was as good as dead.

Lazaro Sanchez was a two-bit bandit who was wanted both sides of the border for murder and rustling. The Bar-H hadn't had trouble with him since they'd run him back across the border for trying to steal their beef. Now he was back.

'Still up to your old tricks I see,' Stanley remarked, trying to show calm.

The Mexican shrugged. 'It is a living.'

'So what happens now?'

'I'm afraid that has already been decided,' Sanchez said trying to sound apologetic. 'You will die and I will take the cattle across the river and sell them. They will not bring much but they will feed the army of the revolution.'

'What are they fightin' about this

time? Who's goin' to take the next bath? Stinkin' Mex killer,' Stanley snarled.

Sanchez's eyes glittered with rage as he took offense to the insult. The Americano was meant to be scared, not showing signs of aggression.

'You talk too much, Gringo,' he snarled and raised his six-gun to shoot Stanley in the head.

★   ★   ★

Something wasn't right. There were too many fresh cattle tracks in the draw and Savage didn't like it. If they remained from the previous roundup a few days before, they wouldn't be as fresh.

Not only that, mixed in with the cow track were the imprints of shod hoofs.

Savage reined in and took the Winchester from the saddle scabbard. He jacked a round into the breech and looked about the draw. Especially the high ground.

It looked clear but his sixth sense told him that there were rustlers about.

Whether they be American or Mexican it didn't matter. To be caught out here alone spelled certain death.

Savage made the decision to find the Bar-H foreman before anything untoward happened.

★ ★ ★

Stanley stiffened when the gunshot came. He cried out in anguish at the prospect of dying. But it wasn't him that had been shot. His eyes snapped open and the scene before him was chaotic.

Sanchez was down in the sandy bottom of the draw, a bright red blossom on the front of his stained jacket and he was twitching his last as death claimed him.

The rustlers scrambled for cover, but weren't quick enough and the rifle fired again. Another bandit screamed as he collapsed with a .44 Henry slug buried deep in his chest.

Stanley cast a glance at the top of the

draw and caught sight of Savage just as his Winchester whip-lashed again, bringing down another bandit.

A wave of relief flooded over Stanley but he knew it wasn't over just yet. There were still two more bandits in the brush.

The Bar-H foreman drew his six-gun and advanced on the brush where the two had disappeared. He could hear them crashing about somewhere ahead of him so he loosed off two shots.

From above, Savage fired again, more in hope than anything else. He caught sight of Stanley about to disappear into the dense thicket and called out.

'Stanley, wait!'

The foreman stopped and looked up at Savage.

'Let 'em go. You can't see much of anythin' in there. All you'll do is get yourself shot.'

Stanley thought hard about what Savage had just told him and knew it made sense.

'OK,' he called back.

'I'll be right down.'

As he waited for Savage, he heard the drumming of retreating hooves and knew that the bandits were now riding hard for the river.

Savage appeared on his sorrel.

'Good thing you appeared when you did,' Stanley allowed. 'I thought I was dead there for a while. Bastards jumped me when I was lookin' over their makeshift corral.'

'They left a heap of fresh sign in the draw I was checkin' out,' Savage explained. 'I figured they were rustlers and thought it would be better if we worked together.'

'Damn fine idea. I owe you a drink when we go to town next payday.'

For a moment Savage forgot why he was there. 'I'll keep you to that.'

★ ★ ★

'I believe I have you to thank for riddin' the state of Texas of a murderous son of a bitch named Sanchez, is that right?'

Savage looked up at the big man standing beside the scuffed table. He wore trail-stained clothes, a battered wide-brimmed hat, and a Texas Rangers badge. He had brown eyes set in a walnut-colored face.

Before he could say anything, Stanley interrupted. 'Hell Butch, He nailed him dead center. If he hadn't, there is no way I would be here talkin' to you as the bastard would have killed me instead.'

The ranger nodded. 'I see. What's your name stranger?'

'Jeff Savage,' Savage answered.

The ranger looked at him thoughtfully. 'Savage huh? Seems to me I've heard that name of late.'

'I doubt it,' Savage responded, trying to deter any more questions.

He looked about the bar room, hoping that would do the trick. Except he locked gazes with Chase Hunter who stood at the long, plain, hardwood bar with his right foot resting on a battered foot-rail.

The scrape of chair legs on plank flooring drew Savage's attention back to his table and he saw that the ranger had sat down.

'My name is Butch Harper by the way,' Harper introduced himself. 'I kind of haunt these parts.'

'Harper's been tryin' to nail Sanchez for the last couple of years,' Stanley explained.

'Almost had him once too,' Harper allowed. 'That was until he slipped through my fingers.'

Harper's gaze lingered on Savage as though he expected him to say something, but the moment was broken by the squeal of a whore as one of the Bar-H cowboys swept her off her feet and onto his lap.

A sudden realization dawned on him and a look of recognition came over Harper's face.

'Now I recall,' he exclaimed. 'You're that feller who's been huntin' Carver and his outlaws. From what I hear, you've been makin' quite a dent in 'em too.'

There was an inquisitive look on Stanley's face as he tried to comprehend what he'd just heard.

And of course, there was no denying it so Savage nodded calmly and said,

'Yeah, that's me.'

It wasn't said overly loud but was clearly audible to the cowboy at the next table. He casually stood up and walked across to the bar beside Chase Hunter. He leaned in close and whispered what he'd just heard.

'The hell you say,' Hunter blurted out loudly as he squared up from the bar to face the table where Savage sat.

Savage saw the movement and was instantly alert. His hand dropped to his holstered Remington.

'Well, I'll . . . ' Harper started but got no further.

'Look out!' Savage shouted a warning and lunged at the ranger.

Chase Hunter's face wore a look of contempt as he drew his six-gun and thumbed back the hammer. The barrel wavered in a drink affected fist. One of the whores who saw what was about to happen screeched with fear.

Savage hit Harper solidly and spilled him from the chair just as the gun in Hunter's hand roared loudly. He heard

165

Harper grunt from the impact of the bullet as they both sprawled onto the hard floor.

The gun sounded again and this time, Savage felt the slug burn into his right side. It left him stunned and he lay on his back beside the fallen ranger, unable to move.

Once more the gun thundered and this time the slug dug splinters from the plank floor near Savage's head. He knew that Hunter would eventually hit him if he stayed where he was.

'Chase, put it down,' Stanley's voice boomed in the room.

Savage heard Hunter curse then the gun fired once more.

This time, Hunter hit his target and Stanley died before his body hit the floor next to Savage, his eyes wide, staring.

With all of his willpower, Savage reached down and drew the Remington. The movement felt sluggish but was far from that. As he brought the gun up he rolled over. The Remington snapped into line and the hammer fell.

The six-gun bucked hard in the palm of his hand and the .44 caliber slug smashed into Hunter's middle. It buried deep and doubled him over. The man's gun fell from his grasp with a thud onto the floor.

Savage struggled to his feet and walked towards the wounded outlaw. There was movement to his left from one of the Bar-H cowhands who tried to draw his own gun.

Savage swiveled the Remington and shot him. The slug hit him dead center and the man fell into a crumpled heap.

'Next one tries drawin' on me gets the same,' he snarled as the pain of his wound started to bite.

A hush descended over the saloon as Savage moved farther forward to stand in front of Hunter. He could feel the blood of his wound running down and soaking his pants.

Hunter looked up at him, hate and pain filled his eyes.

'Why?' he gasped out.

'The woman you bastards took from Summerton,' Savage hissed. 'She was my wife.'

Fear filled Hunter's eyes as Savage raised the Remington.

'No, wait!' Hunter screamed, raising a hand to ward off the shot. 'It wasn't me who did it.'

Savage squeezed the trigger and the room filled with the crash of gunfire one last time.

'You murderin' son of a bitch,' he heard a cowhand grate.

Savage faced him and said, 'He should have thought of the consequences before he joined up with an animal like Carver.'

'You're a liar, Savage,' the same cowhand challenged.

'I don't give a damn what you think,' Savage snapped. 'I'm leavin'.'

A few of the Bar-H hands moved to block his way.

'Let him go,' a voice snapped.

From behind the bar, the barkeep produced a sawed-off greener, both hammers on full cock.

'Any of you fellers try to stop him I'll empty this here coach gun at you,' he warned. 'And you, Mister, get the hell out of here.'

'He killed Chase, Zeke,' the cowhand protested.

'He got what he deserved,' Zeke snapped.

There was a moan of pain as Harper stirred on the floor.

'What about him?' Savage asked.

'I'll take care of him, now get. Once Byron Hunter hears about his son, he'll hunt you down to hell and gone.'

'You tell him what his son did,' Savage snarled. 'And tell him that if he comes after me I'll bury him too.'

'I'll tell him. Get on your horse and go.'

'He's wounded, Zeke,' a whore pointed out.

'He'll be a lot more than that if he stays here.'

Without another word, Savage walked stiffly from the saloon and rode out of Presidio.

169

12

An ashen-faced Byron Hunter stared down at his son's corpse that lay on the mortician's table. He still couldn't believe that his son was dead and furthermore, that the men had allowed the culprit to ride out of town.

'Is there anythin' you want special for the stone, Mr. Hunter?' the hollow-faced John Clemson asked.

Hunter looked at the undertaker and shook his head. 'No, just make it good.'

'I'm sure I can take care of it while you're gone.'

'See that you do,' he said grimly.

Hunter walked outside and stood somberly on the rough-plank board-walk. He looked at the ten riders who waited patiently on their horses. He stepped down into the dusty street and went to mount his bay horse.

'Byron, wait,' a voice halted him as he

was about to climb aboard.

Standing on the boardwalk was a rail-thin man with a badge pinned to his chest.

'What do you want, Henry?' he asked as he turned to face the Presidio sheriff.

'Let him go, Byron,' Henry Bunting ordered. 'It wasn't Savage's fault. Chase fired first.'

A fire blazed in Byron Hunter's eyes. 'He shot him while he was unarmed. In my book that's murder and he'll pay.'

'Chase was no good, Byron,' the Presidio sheriff said plainly. 'The apple didn't fall far from that tree.'

'Shut your mouth,' Hunter snarled.

'I was talkin' to Harper,' Bunting continued. 'Your kid and his friends hit a bank in Summerton on the way south. They killed a passel of folk and took a woman. Savage's wife. They raped and murdered her. Ever heard of Carver's Raiders? Chase was with 'em when they hit Texas. He shot first and wounded Harper and killed Stanley. If he weren't dead I'd have him locked up myself. Like I said, let Savage go.'

Hunter ignored Bunting and climbed into the saddle, the soft creak of leather the only sound. He then looked the Presidio sheriff in the eye and snarled, 'He was still my son.'

With a chorus of shouts and rebel yells, eleven men rode out of Presidio with murder in mind.

*   *   *

'I can tell by the look on your face that it didn't go so well,' Harper observed when Bunting entered the small, well-lit hotel room where the ranger was recuperating.

'Stupid old fool won't hear a bad word about his boy,' Bunting explained. 'He rode out of town with ten of his men. If they catch up to Savage, I'd hate to think what would happen.'

'I'd be more afraid for them, Henry. I have a feeling that Savage can take care of himself.'

'Maybe, but he was wounded when

he rode out of Presidio,' Bunting explained. 'He may even still be carryin' the lead in him.'

Harper sighed loudly. 'Damn it.'

He swept back the covers and grimaced as he swung his legs over the edge of the bed.

'What the hell are you doin'?' Bunting asked Harper.

'If that feller is wounded like you say he's goin' to need a hand against that Bar-H crowd.'

'Hell, Harp, you're wounded yourself,' Bunting pointed out. 'Plus you have no idea where to go.'

'I'll just track Hunter and his men. If they find him then I will too. Now, if you want to help me, get my horse and chuck a saddle on it.'

The sheriff shook his head. If there was one thing he knew about Harper, it was that he was a tough sonuver. And if anyone could stop Hunter, it was him.

The first days of his journey were filled with burning pain as the wound in

Savage's side opened and closed as he rode hard to put distance between himself and Presidio. He did the best he could to keep it clean but the inevitable happened and infection set in.

From then on, everything was a blur of creosote, grass, pinyon, and juniper. Of rock and sand and rattlers and direction.

Which was why, when he awoke, Savage had no idea where he was.

The first thing he noticed was the soft bed he was in. The second was the piercing sunlight that fell through the window to his right and almost blinded him when he opened his eyes.

His immediate reaction, apart from snapping his eyes closed, was to raise his right hand in an attempt to block the glare with his arm. His actions only succeeded to send a bolt of pain throughout his wounded side.

Savage reflexively jerked at it and made his side hurt more. He hissed at the pain and became still, as he waited for it to abate. The moment gave him a chance to look at his surroundings.

The room was small, neatly furnished, and very clean. A woman's touch he presumed.

To his left there was movement and Savage looked to see a small boy, maybe five-years-old filling about a quarter of the large doorway. His lad's eyes widened and he turned to run away. As he went, Savage heard him call out.

'Ma, he's awake,' he shouted. 'Ma, he's awake. He looked at me.'

The boy's excitement was followed by the soft tones of a woman's voice then she appeared in the doorway that the boy had just vacated.

'Jeremy said you were awake,' she said smiling. 'How are you feeling?'

She was tall, around six feet, and was slim built. She had long black hair tied back off her finely featured face. She wore a gray dress that had been cut off just above the floor and a stained, homespun apron.

'I hurt,' he croaked.

She smiled knowingly. 'I'm not surprised. You had a nasty wound and a nasty infection to go with it. The doctor did what he could and said the rest was up to you. I guess you'll live.'

'Where am I?' Savage asked.

'You're on the O'Rielly spread about five miles from Boulder Spring,' she informed him. 'I'm Maddie O'Rielly.'

'I'm Savage.'

'I know,' she smiled again, this time, her face glowed with warmth. 'You talked a lot.'

Savage felt a flush of embarrassment touch his cheeks and he tried to divert it by asking, 'How long have I been here?'

'Five days.'

Silence followed and then Maddie asked, 'Are you hungry?'

At the mention of food, Savage realized that he could eat and nodded. 'Yeah, that would be great. I think.'

'I'll fix you something to eat.'

He watched her go and then he closed his eyes and attempted to piece together past events but it was all too foggy.

'Hello.'

Savage opened his eyes and saw the small boy.

'I'm Jeremy,' he said by way of introduction. 'Who are you?'

'I'm Jeff.'

'Hey, your name starts with a J too.'

Savage smiled at Jeremy's genuine excitement. 'I suppose it does.'

'What happened to you?'

'I had a little trouble.'

'My Pa always said you should steer clear of trouble.'

Savage smiled. 'He's a wise man. Where is your Pa, I'd like to talk to him.'

Jeremy's face fell. 'He died. He was shot too.'

Savage cursed inwardly. 'I'm sorry, son. So who looks after the ranch?'

'Ma does.'

'All by herself?'

'No, not all by myself,' Maddie said from where she was standing in the doorway. 'I have hands that work for me. Is there something wrong with that?'

Savage noticed the defiant look in her eyes and said quickly, 'No, ma'am. No problem at all. I meant nothing by it.'

'Good,' she said brusquely. 'Jeremy, come and leave Mr. Savage alone. Let him get some more rest.'

The boy was about to protest but the look on his mother's face prevented it. Instead, he hurried from the room.

'I'm sorry . . . ' Savage started to apologize but Maddie cut him off.

'Your food will be ready shortly,' she said curtly and walked away.

★   ★   ★

'Smells good,' Savage said, startling Maddie as she stood at the stove.

She whirled and looked at him. 'My Lord. What are you doing out of bed?'

Savage shrugged. It had taken a little effort but he'd managed.

'I see you found your clothes.'

'Yes, thanks for fixin' 'em up.'

'You'd better sit down before you

fall,' Maddie said and pulled out a chair at the polished dining room table.

The room was large and like the bedroom, it was spotlessly clean. The aroma of the frying food permeated it.

Savage moved forward and was about to sit down when Jeremy came running inside. The screen door crashed back as he burst through the doorway.

'There're riders comin' in Ma,' he said excitedly. 'Strangers I think.'

A worried expression passed over Maddie O'Rielly's face.

Savage walked across to the window and peered out. There were eleven riders in all and out front he recognized the familiar form of Byron Hunter.

He turned and faced Maddie. 'Where are my guns?'

'Why? Who are they?'

'They're after me,' Savage said hurriedly. 'The feller leadin' 'em is Byron Hunter. I killed his son.'

'You what?' Maddie blurted out as her voice rose.

'Maddie, I need my guns,' Savage

said with authority. 'Trust me when I say there was no choice. His son was bad. He was part of a bunch of outlaws that . . . '

'Amy?' Maddie said as a piece of the puzzle from Savage's delirious ramblings fell into place.

'Yes, my wife,' Savage confirmed.

'Jeremy get Mr. Savage his guns. And then hide in your room and don't come out until I call you.'

The boy scurried off and Savage said, 'What about your hands?'

'They're out working the Shallow Creek range,' Maddie told him. 'They're too far away to be of any help.'

Jeremy returned with the holstered Remington and the Yellow Boy. He gave them to Savage and disappeared again.

Maddie walked towards the door.

'What are you doin'?' Savage asked.

'I'm going out there to talk to them,' she answered.

'What?'

'I have a little boy in the other room who is all I have left in this world,' she explained. 'If I can stop this before it starts then I'm more than happy to try.'

Before Savage could protest further she was gone.

He made sure the Winchester and Remington were loaded and moved over to the doorway where he remained out of sight and waited to see what would ensue.

★　★　★

The riders halted in the center of the O'Rielly ranch-yard amid a cloud of dust and a cacophony of stamping hoofs and loud snorts. One of the riders broke off from the group and went across to the corral near the barn.

Maddie stepped down confidently from the veranda and walked towards them.

'Can I help you gentlemen?' she asked.

'Is your husband around?' Byron Hunter asked abruptly.

'No, he isn't Mr . . . ?'

'The name's Hunter,' he told her

181

impatiently. 'Seein' as your man ain't around you'll have to do. We're lookin' for a murderer by the name of Savage. Have you seen him?'

'There is no one here by that name, Mr. Hunter.'

'I guess we'll see won't we,' he said looking across at the lone rider.

Alarm shot through her when she realized that the sorrel was still in the corral.

'I've told you what you want to know now get off my land,' Maddie snapped.

'We'll leave when we're sure that he's not here,' Hunter snapped. 'And not before.'

Maddie grew even more nervous as she looked at the grime-covered men on their horses. Then she turned her attention to the lone cowhand who was now coming back.

'His sorrel is in the corral, Mr. Hunter,' he said. 'I'd know it anywhere.'

Hunter turned his gaze on Maddie who could see that his face was a mask of anger at being lied to.

'It would seem that you are not tellin' us the truth,' he said harshly. 'Where the hell is he?'

'He's not here,' she responded defiantly.

'I asked you a question damn it,' Hunter roared. 'Tell me where he is.'

'I don't know.'

Byron Hunter came off his horse with eyes blazing with fury. He crossed the short distance to Maddie O'Rielly and grabbed her arm in a vice-like grip as she turned to run.

'Where the hell do you think you're goin'?'

'Let her go, Hunter,' Savage's voice cracked across the yard.

The rancher looked across to where Savage stood on the veranda, holding the Yellow Boy.

'So we've finally caught you,' Hunter sneered. 'Put the rifle down or I'll have my men shoot you where you stand.'

'You do that,' Savage shot back. 'You, however, won't get the satisfaction of seein' it. 'Cause you'll be the first person to die. You may not be the last either.'

'Are you willin' to take a chance on the woman's life Savage?'

'She ain't got nothin' to do with it, Hunter,' Savage told him. 'Leave her be. Your quarrel is with me.'

'I tell you what, if you put down the rifle then I'll let the woman go. If you don't then she dies.'

With a swift movement, Hunter ducked in behind Maddie and drew his Colt from its holster. He pressed it hard against the side of her head.

Hunter smiled coldly. 'Your choice.'

13

Savage was beaten and he knew it. He didn't have a clear shot and even if he tried, he would be condemning Maddie to death and Jeremy to a life without parents.

He looked into her eyes and saw her silent plea.

There was no other option.

The rifle clattered onto the veranda as Savage let it go. 'There, you got what you wanted. Now let her go.'

'The six-shooter too,' Hunter ordered.

Savage unbuckled the gun belt and let it fall.

'Now step forward into the yard.'

Once he was out in the middle of the yard, Hunter gave his men a signal and they came off their horses and closed in around him.

'I guess it don't mean much to you boys that Chase shot Stanley down, huh?' Savage commented.

'That was an accident,' Hunter snapped.

'And Harper?'

'The same.'

'And the fact that he was a yellow dog and murderer who rapes women?'

'He was my son!' Hunter raged.

'He got what he deserved!'

'Somebody get a rope,' the rage-crazed rancher snapped. 'We're goin' to hang the bastard right now.'

'No!' Maddie cried.

Hunter released her and pushed her away. She staggered briefly then hurried to stand in front of Savage.

'You can't do it. It'll be murder.'

'It's no less than what he did to my son,' Hunter barked. 'Now get out of the way.'

Maddie felt Savage's hand on her shoulder. 'It's OK. Go inside and take care of Jeremy.'

She whirled around and stared into his eyes. 'I can't.'

'If you don't, they'll kill you too.

What will Jeremy do then?' Savage said gently.

Maddie held his gaze for what seemed like an age. He saw the pain of being powerless in her pale-blue eyes. Then she stepped around him and walked towards the house.

'Right, get him up on a horse and . . . ' Hunter looked about until he found what he wanted. 'And get the rope over the arch above the gateway.'

Five minutes later a cowhand known as Scott settled the noose over Savage's head and drew the knot up snug.

'Any last words, Killer?' Hunter asked with a hint of satisfaction in his voice.

Savage remained silent, staring straight ahead.

'No?'

'I do,' a voice boomed across the ranch yard. 'The law takes a mighty dim view of lynchin' an innocent man.'

All eyes turned to stare at the man who'd appeared from around the corner of the plank-walled barn holding a leveled Henry rifle.

'What do you want here, Harper?' Hunter challenged. 'You're interruptin'.'

'I'll start shootin' if you don't cut Savage down from there right pronto,' Harper warned them.

Hunter turned scarlet. 'He killed . . . '

'A murderin' son of a bitch,' Harper said scathingly. 'Now cut him down.'

Scott reached over and took the noose from around Savage's neck. After which he cut the bindings from his wrists.

Harper walked further into the yard while Scott cut Savage loose.

'You should have left it alone, Harper,' Hunter growled, his voice edgy with menace.

'I tell you what, Byron,' Harper began, 'I'll forget about arrestin' you on false imprisonment and attempted murder charges and all you gotta do is mount up and ride out.'

'And if I don't?'

'Then I'll shoot you. Plain and simple.'

Savage tensed as the air became electrified with tension. Hunter stood firm where he was, trembling with rage, his hard gaze locked on that of Harper's.

'What's it goin' to be?'

Byron Hunter's shoulders slumped in defeat and he turned away from Harper. He looked at his men and ordered, 'Mount up, we're leavin'.'

What happened next took everyone by surprise. For a man of his age, Byron Hunter moved quite quickly as his hand clawed at the butt of the Colt in his holster.

Hunter's scowl turned into a look of triumph as the six-gun came up level and he squeezed the trigger. The gun bucked and roared. Flame spewed from its barrel amid the puff of gray-blue gun smoke.

The shot, however, missed, and triumph turned to terror as Harper brought the Henry into line from the hip and snapped off a shot.

Byron Hunter's mouth flew wide as the .44 caliber slug punched into his chest. It flattened as it smashed through a rib and destroyed everything in its path before exploding in a spray of crimson from the rancher's back.

Harper levered and fired again, the second shot knocked Hunter to the hard-packed earth of the ranch yard. The older man lay on his back, sightless eyes stared at the cloudless sky overhead.

Harper levered another round into the Henry's breech and brought it to bear on the Bar-H hands.

'Don't any of you try anythin',' he snarled. 'It's over. Get on your horses and skedaddle. And take your boss with you.'

Savage and Harper watched them carefully as they loaded Hunter onto his horse. They then climbed onto their own mounts and rode away.

Savage turned to Harper and said gratefully, 'Thanks for savin' my neck.'

Harper nodded and was about to speak when his attention was diverted to the ranch house as Maddie and Jeremy emerged.

'Are you OK?' Maddie asked him.

'I wouldn't be if Harper hadn't come along.'

Savage introduced them and then said, 'Maddie looked after me when I showed up loaded with infection from the bullet Chase put in me.'

Harper nodded. 'Pleased to meet you, Ma'am.'

'Likewise.'

Harper went on to explain how he happened to be there, then later, when they were all inside he asked, 'Where to now? I take it you're goin' to continue with this quest of yours?'

'New Mexico,' Savage explained. 'Cody said that was where Carver and the other two were headed.'

'I'd like to help you but my jurisdiction sort of runs out at the border,' Harper said sounding almost apologetic that he couldn't help.

'It's somethin' I have to do on my own,' Savage told him. 'I had a chance in the war to do it and I failed. People died ... Amy died because of that failure. Now I have to make it right.'

'Why?' Maddie blurted out.

The two men looked at her as she sat across the dining room table from them.

'Because it has to be done,' Savage answered.

'But why you?' she asked. 'Why does it have to be you? Do you think your wife would want you to go on like this? You could stay here, I need another hand.'

Savage shook his head gently. 'No, but thanks for the offer. I appreciate everythin' you've done for me already but I'll be ridin' on in a few days once I feel stronger. I'll ride into town and get some supplies then head for New Mexico.'

Maddie stared at him open-mouthed for a brief moment before she stood up and stomped from the room.

'I think she had hopes for you,' Harper observed.

'She's lonely,' Savage explained. 'Her man died a while back and now she runs the ranch and looks after the boy.'

'You *could* stay,' Harper surmised.
'No, I couldn't.'

*   *   *

Harper rode out the following day after sleeping in the barn for the night. He was heading back to Presidio to take care of a few things, at least that was his excuse.

The next few days for Savage were spent trying to regain his strength and he put himself to work around the ranch yard. Forever under the watchful eye of Jeremy.

The night before the fourth day, Savage decided that he was ready to continue his search. The next morning he rode out before the first orange fingers of dawn streaked the Texas sky. As a departing gift, he'd left behind half of the money from Wheeler tucked under a plate on the dining-room table.

*   *   *

Savage bought provisions in Boulder Spring and continued to ride for the next two days. On the third day, he rode into the town of Desert Wells. Not an overly large town with five-hundred citizens, but a prosperous one nonetheless.

The trail came down off a low ridge, passed a small chapel with a graveyard and when it hit the edge of town, became a long main street.

The main street itself was lined with a mix of false-fronted shops and adobe structures. There were three saloons, The Cactus Juice, The Watering Hole, and The Longhorn.

Besides those, there was a blacksmith, gunsmith, land office, assayer, barber, two general stores, a diner, stage and freight office, jail, a hotel, and at the far end of town was the Sparkling Kitty. A house of ill-repute. There too he found the livery stables with a large corral out back.

Once the sorrel was seen to, Savage walked back along the plank boardwalk until he reached the hotel. Above the windows of the second floor was a large hand-painted sign with bold red lettering saying, **Desert Wells Hotel.**

Savage paused briefly to toss the saddlebags over his right shoulder and transfer the Winchester into his right hand. Using his left he pushed open the hotel door and walked in . . .

. . . to trouble, head-on.

* ★ ★

Upon entry to the hotel's broad, well-lit foyer, what greeted Savage was the sight of a man slapping the desk clerk down. The man had taken several blows by the look of the blood on his face and as the hand rose again, Savage said in a low, clear voice, 'I wouldn't if I were you.'

The sweeping blow stopped mid-swing and the slim man with brown hair hidden away under a battered Confederate campaign hat turned slowly and deliberately.

He stared at the bearded man clad in

195

Union blue and buckskin, who dared challenge him before he said, 'You're new here Stranger, so this time I'll let it slide. But just so you know, don't get caught up in somethin' that ain't your affair. We don't cotton to nosy Blue-bellies.'

'And what if I make it my affair?'

The man pulled his jacket aside and revealed a tarnished deputy sheriff's badge.

Savage nodded. 'So that gives you the power to do what you want?'

'If you stick around long enough, you'll find out,' he sneered.

Confidently he turned back to face the clerk and raised his hand to slap him.

In a fluid movement, Savage closed the gap between himself and the deputy and brought up the Yellow Boy and drove the butt into his kidney area.

The deputy cried out and stiffened. Then sank to his knees as the pain of the blow traveled throughout his body.

The Yellow Boy arced again. This

time, it cracked against bone and opened up a gash in the scalp at the back of the deputy's head. Soundlessly, he slumped forward and didn't move.

'Are you OK?'

The clerk nodded. He was a flabby man with a bulbous nose which was dripping red onto his once clean shirt. Suddenly his expression changed and his eyes grew wide.

'You have to go,' he blurted out in a panic. 'You can't stay, you have to leave.'

Savage frowned. 'I only just got here and I want a room.'

The clerk glanced at the deputy and then back to the stranger who stood in front of him. 'You don't understand, he's a deputy.'

'What do you mean? Surely the sheriff won't let him get away . . . '

'The sheriff is behind it all,' the stricken man blurted out. 'You must go or they'll kill you.'

It dawned on Savage that the man was serious. He was genuinely scared.

He shrugged and turned to leave but the doorway was blocked by a man armed with a coach gun, its hammers back on full cock. The solidly built man stood six-foot-three, had blond hair and ice-blue eyes set in a square-jawed face. The face was one he recognized instantly.

The man in the doorway wore a shiny badge with the word **Sheriff** stamped on it. It was John Carver. The man he'd come all this way to kill.

14

An evil smile split the Sheriff's cruel lips as he asked, 'Goin' somewhere?'

Internally, Savage was a whole whirlpool of emotion, an overwhelming urge to kill this man bubbled to the surface. He knew that such an attempt would be useless as Carver would drop the hammers of the shotgun. And Savage would die for nothing.

He fought his natural compunctions and remained silent, then waited to see what would happen next.

There was a moan from behind Savage as the deputy started to stir.

'Mind tellin' me what happened?' Carver asked in a low voice.

'Your deputy was up on the desk clerk,' Savage explained. 'He seemed to think that the badge he had pinned to his chest gave him the power to do so.'

'And?'

Savage shrugged casually. 'He was wrong.'

'So you took it upon yourself to assault a peace officer in the act of doin' his duty?'

'If his *duty* as you call it is beatin' up defenseless townsfolk then yeah, I did that.'

Something dawned on Savage. If Carver was here wearing a badge, then it was a fair bet that the groaning deputy was one of Carver's gang too. That would make him either Thomas or Cooper. He had no idea which but reckoned that if two of them were in Desert Wells, then the last one was probably here too.

Slowly, the deputy came around and climbed to his feet. He massaged his back and gingerly touched his split scalp opened up by the blow. When he took his hand away it was sticky with blood.

The deputy's face screwed up as he looked at Savage and hissed, 'You stinkin' son of a bitch.'

He made to grab at his holstered six-gun but a snapped order from Carver stayed his hand.

'Save it.'

The deputy looked at him defiantly. 'We should just kill him now.'

Carver shook his head. 'No. We'll make an example of him. Take his guns and go get that head looked at. I'll lock him up.'

The deputy grunted and relieved Savage of the Yellow Boy and the Remington. After which he was marched off to jail under the watchful eye of a killer.

* * *

The answer to Savage's lingering question was answered as they walked into the small jail. Behind the scarred desk, also wearing a deputy badge, was the third and final outlaw. A lean, boyish-faced young man with brown hair.

'What's goin' on?' he asked Carver who shoved Savage through the door.

'Didn't Ringo tell you what was

happenin'?' Carver asked.

There it was. He'd hit Ringo Thomas.

'He just mumbled somethin' about wantin' to kill some stranger and you not lettin' him.'

'That's right,' Carver allowed. 'We're goin' to hang him for the whole town to see. It's time we reminded them who's in charge.'

'Do the town's people actually know who you lot really are?' Savage inquired.

Both men stared blankly at him before Carver turned to the gun rack and stowed the coach gun.

'What do you mean?' he asked suspiciously.

'Well, you fellers are obviously not who the town thought you were,' Savage answered. 'If they knew, I doubt you would have gotten a toe hold here. And now it's too late.'

'How does he know?' Cooper asked.

'He don't know nothin',' Carver said gruffly.

'John Carver ex-raider, murderer and all-around son of a bitch,' Savage stated and turned to face the stricken Cooper. 'You're Cooper, same type of scum as your boss. The feller I hit is Thomas. Again, cut from the same mold. You all are the last three.'

'The last three what?' Carver asked.

'The last three that I have to kill,' Savage explained. 'The rest are dead.'

Carver raised his eyebrows. 'By your hand?'

'Mostly.'

Carver stared thoughtfully at Savage.

'We need to kill him now before the rest of the town finds out who we are,' Cooper declared.

Carver raised his hand to silence Cooper and the outlaw shut down. The killer's gaze lingered then his eyes flickered with a hint of recognition.

'I have a feelin' that hiding under that beard is a face I've seen before,' Carver pondered. 'Am I right?'

'Shenandoah Valley, '64,' Savage answered.

Puzzled, Carver said, 'Refresh my memory. Tell me your name.'

'My name is Savage. I was in charge of the cavalry patrol that all but wiped out your bunch of killers,' Savage elaborated.

A strange expression came over Carver's face. One of recognition, hatred, and admiration.

'Now I remember, I shot you. And yet here you are, still alive.'

Savage remained silent.

'But why would a man I shot so long ago be here now trackin' and killin' all of my men?' Carver inquired. 'Unless . . . unless there was another reason.'

Still, Savage said nothing.

Carver raised his eyebrows. 'Nothing to say?'

Still nothing.

'Lock him up, Coop,' Carver snarled.

'I still say we should kill him now,' Cooper reiterated.

'Just do it,' Carver snapped. 'And then find someone to build a gallows.'

'Where do you want it built?'

'In the middle of the main damned street.'

Later that evening, the three outlaws gathered around the desk and discussed Savage. Thomas and Cooper demanded that Carver kill him straight away but Carver remained defiant.

'He'll die when I want him to and not before,' Carver said with finality. 'He intrigues me and I want to find out why he's gone to such trouble to find us.'

'And what if the town finds out our real names?' Thomas asked.

'Then we move on and set up somewhere else.'

They were not happy with the decision but Carver let them know in certain terms that he was still in charge and would not be questioned further on the matter.

* * *

It took three days for the gallows to be built. It would have taken two but progress was hampered by rain on the second day. All day, a steady drizzle had fallen from the leaden sky and turned the dust and dirt of the main street into a sticky mess.

On the evening of the third day, Carver entered the office with a smile. He walked out the back to the cells and stopped in front of the iron bars of Savage's temporary home.

Savage sat on a lumpy mattress that covered a steel-framed cot.

'Tomorrow you'll swing,' Carver boasted. 'The whole town will turn out to see it happen.'

'Why would they do that?'

'Because they were told to.'

'Just like that?'

'Yes, just like that.'

'Aren't you afraid I'll say somethin'?' Savage asked the smirking killer.

'Not in the least,' Carver said confidently. 'You'll be wearing a hood and a gag.'

Savage fell silent once again.

'Tell me why,' Carver said.

'Why what?'

'Why you're here of course,' Carver said with an inquisitive tone. Savage said only one word. 'Summerton.'

'Were you there?'

'No.'

'So again, why?'

'Because you and your scum took my wife and killed her,' Savage spat. 'But only after you'd had your fun.'

'So that's why,' Carver nodded and then said coldly, 'It was fun too.'

For the first time since they'd locked him up, Savage lost his composure and flew at the bars, startling Carver.

'I'll kill you, you son of a bitch!' he shouted. 'I'll damn well kill you!'

'If you manage to get out of there before tomorrow, come and find me,' Carver smirked and turned away, then strode purposefully towards the office door.

As Savage watched him go, he mumbled an incoherent promise. 'You're dead you bastard. I'll get out of here and when I do you're dead.'

15

'Hey!' Savage shouted for the fifth time. 'Hey, is there anybody out there?'

When no one came he picked up the empty tin mug and started to run it back and forth along the iron bars.

He kept it up for around a minute before Cooper threw open the office door and shouted, 'Shut the hell up and stop that racket!'

'I need to go to the privy,' Savage growled at him.

'Too bad,' Cooper snapped. 'Wait until the morning. I'm on my own.'

'If you don't let me go I'll drop my drawers and take a dump right here in the middle of the damned floor,' Savage said as he grimaced and rubbed his belly. 'I think there was somethin' wrong with the food.'

'Not goin' to happen,' Cooper said.

'What do you think your boss will say

if he comes in here tomorrow mornin'
and there's a big pile of shit in here?
Are you going to want to clean it up?'

A look of uncertainty swept over
Cooper's face but the outlaw remained
unmoved.

'Well come on man, make up your
mind. I can't wait all night.'

Still, Cooper made no move.

'What the hell,' Savage said and
shrugged his shoulders before starting
to fumble with his belt buckle.

'Hey, wait,' Cooper blurted out.
'Alright, I'll take you. I'll just get the
keys.'

Savage watched him disappear and
after a brief period return with the keys
and coach gun. The keys rattled in the
door lock and the door swung open
with a screech.

Cooper stepped back and raised the
gun. 'If you try anythin' funny, I'll
unload both barrels into you.'

Savage walked out the back door and
into the crisp night air of the desert.
There was no cloud cover to speak of

and the moon cast its silvery glow across the town. Far off in the distance, he could hear the yip of a coyote.

The stab of the gun barrels in his back prodded Savage to move.

The privy was a small, foul-smelling, plank-built blight that stood near a pile of split wood around thirty feet from the back door of the jail. As he got close, Savage staggered and went down on one knee. He cursed the dark, and a small rut in the path.

The coach gun prodded him again. 'Get up and move.'

As Savage rose, he scooped up a handful of loose soil which he flung at Cooper's face. As the outlaw reeled back, Savage continued the arc of his swing and grasped for the coach gun. His left hand clamped down on the twin hammers so the weapon couldn't be fired.

With his right hand, he chopped down on Cooper's arm and broke the man's grip on the gun. Cooper cried out with pain.

Savage dropped the coach gun and continued his attack. His right fist darted out swiftly and he punched Cooper in the throat. The outlaw gagged and clutched at the affected area. He tried to call out but his damaged throat emitted only a hoarse gasp.

As he moved in closer, Savage smashed two blows to the outlaw's face. There was a sickening crunch as Cooper's jaw broke and blood began to flow freely from his wrecked mouth. His legs buckled and he collapsed to the ground. Savage drew back his right boot and drove a furious kick into Cooper's head. There was a loud smack of leather on bone and the outlaw ceased all movement.

He blew out a harsh breath then glanced about to see if anyone had witnessed the savage exchange. When he saw no one, he hurried back inside the jail.

The cell area was clear and he cautiously approached the office door then eased it open a crack and looked through. It too was vacant.

Savage strode into the office and found what he was looking for. The Winchester was in the gun rack and the Remington was in the top drawer of the desk. His saddlebags still sat in a dusty corner of the room where they'd been dropped.

The remainder of his money was tucked away in his boot. He had everything he needed, so it was time to send Carver a message and let him know that this thing was far from over.

★　★　★

An ashen-faced Ringo Thomas crashed his fist repeatedly on the closed door of Carver's room at the Sparkling Kitty the following morning.

A slim red-headed whore, with a smattering of freckles and a blackened eye, stirred beside Carver as the drumming continued.

Annoyed at being rudely awoken, Carver dragged himself from the bed which groaned and squeaked in protest of the movements. He scooped up one of his Colts from the bedside table and padded across to the door with not a stitch on.

'Who is it?' he asked gruffly.

'It's me,' Thomas answered.

'What time is it?'

'Just after dawn,' Thomas informed him. 'Damn it open up.'

Carver turned away from the door. 'Go away.'

The door crashed back and Thomas' frame filled the doorway. The redhead whore in the bed shot up, eyes wide with fright. Carver was about to explode with rage when he saw the look on Thomas' face.

'What is it?' he asked cautiously.

'You'd better get your duds on and come with me,' Thomas said grimly.

That told him that it must be bad. 'I'll be right out.'

Carver dressed hurriedly and rushed out the door to find Thomas still waiting.

'Are you goin' to tell me what this is about?' he asked Thomas as he followed him along a narrow hallway.

'You need to see it,' Thomas told him. 'And trust me, you ain't goin' to like it.'

*   *   *

Outside, the orange of the new day had appeared but the sun was yet to make its long climb into the sky. Though it was early, there was nobody about, instead, it was eerily quiet. Nothing moved along the street, not even the usual morning breeze that came off the desert after sun-up.

Carver frowned at the stillness. Then he saw the scaffold in the distance and remembered that today was the day set to hang Savage. He did a double take as there appeared to be a body already hanging from the rope.

He looked at Thomas questioningly. 'What the hell is that?'

'That's Cooper,' Thomas told him.

Carver was stunned. 'What? How?'

'Savage killed him,' Thomas explained. 'He hung him there as a message for you.'

'What makes you say that?'

'A man don't have to be a genius to figure it out. Not after what we done to his wife.'

Carver stepped down off the boardwalk and out into the main street. He made his slow and cautious way towards the scaffold, acutely aware of the dozens of eyes that peered out through windows, watching to see what their self-anointed sheriff would do next.

Ahead of the two outlaws, there was a flutter of black as a crow swooped down and landed on top of Cooper's head. It cawed an invitation to unseen friends then leaned down over the dead outlaw's forehead, and drove its beak into the left eye.

It worked briefly then flapped its wings and flew off over the top of the false-fronted buildings with its grisly trophy.

Thirty yards later, Carver and Thomas stood at the base of the scaffold and looked up at the blackened, misshapen face that belonged to Cooper. The trap hadn't been tripped. The rope was hauled up short so that Cooper's feet dangled just above the platform.

Carver noticed a piece of paper sticking out of Cooper's shirt pocket and knew that it was meant for him. He pointed it out to Thomas and asked, 'Did you see that before?'

Thomas shook his head. 'Nope.'

Carver dropped his hand to his right-side six-gun and looked about the street. At a glance, it appeared to be clear and when he turned back, Thomas had moved around the pine-built structure towards the steps.

He climbed them cautiously and when he'd reached the platform he stopped in front of the dangling corpse.

Thomas wrinkled his nose at the stench of the corpse, wherein death, the body had defecated. For a man who'd been surrounded by so much death in recent years, it was a smell he knew well but would never grow used to.

He reached out tentatively and drew the piece of paper from Cooper's pocket. As he unfolded it, he turned away from the corpse.

Thomas read the note then suddenly focused his gaze on Carver, a mortified expression on his face.

'What is it?' Carver snapped.

That was when Thomas' head seemed to explode.

16

Savage had watched them come along the main street from his position behind a curtain on the second floor of The Desert Wells Hotel.

He jacked a round into the Yellow Boy's breech and slid the barrel out of the window and waited.

Word had quickly spread throughout the town about the happenings of the night before, helped along by the mouth of the hotel's desk clerk. The town collectively held its breath in anticipation, knowing full well that the only way to rid their town of the killers was with bloody violence.

Savage waited as Carver and Thomas stopped short of the scaffold and looked at Cooper. There was a brief discussion and Thomas walked around to the scaffold and climbed the steps.

As Savage sighted along the rifle's

barrel, Thomas read the note and glanced at Carver.

The Yellow Boy roared in the confines of the small room and the Winchester slammed back against Savage's shoulder. Without waiting to see if his first shot had hit its target he worked the lever and shifted his aim to Carver.

Once more the Yellow Boy spat flame and Carver collapsed as his right leg went out from underneath him.

* * *

As the echoes of the first shot died away, Thomas fell from the scaffold and landed on his back at Carver's feet with a sickening thud. The outlaw was missing a large chunk of his skull from where the .44 caliber slug had blown it away, his sightless eyes stared at the cloudless sky.

Something else caught the eye of a stunned Carver. The note fluttered down and landed in the dust beside Thomas' corpse. It was right-side up and the outlaw was able to read the large, hand-written message Savage had left.

It said: **You're next!**

The rifle roared again and Carver felt the hammer-blow of the slug as it tore through his upper thigh. He collapsed to the ground, a temporary numbness took away any pain.

But it didn't last long as a burning sensation started to radiate outwards from the ghastly wound. He grasped at his leg and attempted to staunch the flow of blood as the wash of crimson spread across the material of his pants. But even as he did so, a small pool started to form beneath him in the dirt.

Panic began to build in Carver as it suddenly dawned on him that he was vulnerable. He grasped at one of his Colts. Fingers, slick with blood, fumbled with it before he managed to get it out of its holster.

Carver eased back the hammer and frantically looked for a target to shoot at.

★   ★   ★

Savage strode purposefully out onto the boardwalk and stepped down onto the street. He changed the Yellow Boy into his left hand and palmed up his Remington. Ahead of him, at the base of the scaffold, lay Carver, with his six-gun drawn, desperately looking for Savage.

When he saw Savage walking towards him, Carver's eyes grew wide with alarm and he brought the Colt up to fire.

The Remington blazed and a .44 slug punched into Carver's gun-arm. The bullet broke his arm and his fingers opened reflexively, and he dropped the unfired Colt. He cried out in pain and a thin sheen of sweat appeared on his forehead.

Savage continued to approach him at a steady pace. The heels of his cavalry boots left small scuff marks in the dust.

Carver grabbed urgently at his second gun but only had it halfway out when another shot from Savage smashed that arm too.

Now, overcome with pain, Carver flopped onto his back. He seemed defeated as the realization of his imminent demise finally took hold.

He fought back the urge to cry out as the waves of pain washed over him.

From the other side of fly-specked glass, townsfolk watched expectantly as Savage drew closer to the wounded killer.

And then he was there. Carver looked up to see the man standing over him, staring down with hate filled eyes. His Remington was pointed at the killer's head.

A sudden wave of calmness gripped Carver and he raised his head and smiled wryly. 'I guess this is it then, huh?'

The Remington roared and a round hole appeared in Carver's forehead. His head smacked against the street, driven back by the impact, sightless eyes open and mouth hanging slack.

It was over. All of Carver's raiders were dead. And the hell of it all was that none of it would bring Amy back.

Townsfolk began to emerge on both sides of the street. Relieved murmurs rippled through the gathering crowd as they realized that the reign of terror forced upon them by those men was finally over. The bandits who had held their town to ransom were all dead.

Savage looked about at the people as they waited to see what he would do next. He looked down at the Remington which was still in his hand.

Silently Savage slipped it back into his holster, brought the Yellow Boy up to rest on his shoulder and began to walk back to the hotel where he'd left his saddlebags.

'Excuse me, Mr. Savage?'

Savage looked to his left and saw a short, thin man who wore a suit and spectacles emerge from the crowd. He stepped down to the street and approached hesitantly.

'What do you want?' asked Savage unpleasantly. Hell, it was all unpleasant.

'My name is Thaddeus Miller. I'm

the mayor,' Miller explained.

'So?'

'May I ask what . . . ?' he paused. 'I mean . . . what is it you plan on doing now?'

'I'm getting my stuff and my horse and leaving.'

'Umm . . . would you consider staying? We need law and order and you could be just the man to do the job.'

Savage glanced about and then brought his gaze back to the mayor. 'No.'

Before Miller could try to persuade him further, Savage pushed past and kept walking.

He'd not thought about what he'd do after achieving his goal of bringing Amy's killers to justice. But he knew that he sure as hell wasn't staying here.

Savage collected his saddlebags and went along to the livery to get the sorrel. He tried to pay the livery man who held up his hand.

'Don't bother, Savage,' he told him. 'After what you've done for the town I ain't goin' to take your money.'

'Thanks,' Savage acknowledged the gesture.

After the sorrel was saddled, he walked it out to the front of the livery stable and mounted. He looked both ways. To the right would take him back to nightmares he wished to forget. To the left . . .

There was movement beside him as the hostler came out and stopped next to the sorrel.

He looked up at Savage and asked, 'What are you goin' to do now?'

Savage heeled the horse forward and turned it left. Without looking back he answered the hostler's question. 'Drift!'

We do hope that you have enjoyed reading this large print book.

Did you know that all of our titles are available for purchase?

We publish a wide range of high quality large print books including:
Romances, Mysteries, Classics
General Fiction
Non Fiction and Westerns

Special interest titles available in large print are:
The Little Oxford Dictionary
Music Book, Song Book
Hymn Book, Service Book

Also available from us courtesy of Oxford University Press:
Young Readers' Dictionary
(large print edition)
Young Readers' Thesaurus
(large print edition)

For further information or a free brochure, please contact us at:
Ulverscroft Large Print Books Ltd.,
The Green, Bradgate Road, Anstey,
Leicester, LE7 7FU, England.
Tel: (00 44) **0116 236 4325**
Fax: (00 44) **0116 234 0205**

COLTER'S QUEST

Neil Hunter

1622: An expedition of Spanish soldiers, carrying a hoard of gold and silver, loses its way in the mountains. Now the last man alive, Father Ignacio Corozon, hides the treasure in a cave . . . 1842: Josiah Colter stumbles across that very same cave and discovers the cache . . . 1888: Josiah's grandson Ben has his home burned to the ground, his wife kidnapped, and his friend killed. Chet Ballard and Jess McCall set out alongside him to find Rachel and avenge the murder . . .

THE KILLING OF JERICHO SLADE

Paxton Johns

When Jericho Slade, the five-year-old son of Senator Morton J. Slade, is killed in Dodge City, someone's neck is bound to be stretched. Billie Flint makes a likely suspect — but when Born Gallant drifts into Dodge and sees the innocence on the accused's face, he reacts impulsively and snatches young Flint from certain death. Setting out to hunt down the real killer of the child, Gallant will soon learn that being the hero does not always mean doing what's right . . .

THE SILVER TRAIL

Ben Bridges

Carter O'Brien's gun is for hire, but only when the job — and the money — is right. As tough as they come, he's been everything from lawman to bounty hunter in his time. Right now he's riding shotgun on an expedition led by an old Army buddy. The goal: to find a lost canyon of silver down in Mexico. But the way is blocked not only by gunmen working for a greedy businessman, but also a ghost from O'Brien's past.

SNOWBOUND

Logan Winters

Private enquiry agent Carson Banner has been hired to track down Julian Prince's missing daughters — Candice, who has eloped with the no-good swindler Bill Saxon; and Ruth, who refused to let her younger sister go off alone with strangers. As a snowstorm out of Canada blows its way south across Dakota land, Banner must find the party before harm comes to the girls — or the blizzards kill them all . . .

RUTHLESS MEN

Corba Sunman

Provost Captain Slade Moran hunts down Private Daniel Green, a deserter from the 2nd Cavalry accused of murder. But, when arrested, Green swears he's innocent. Upon returning to the fort with his prisoner, Moran is informed that trouble has flared up in nearby Lodgepole, where a saloon gambler has been caught cheating and soldiers want revenge. Three men have already roughed up the cardsharp, and now the saloon has caught fire. All suspicion points towards the soldiers of Fort Collins . . .